Death and Deception

Death and Deception

Ray Alan

ROBERT HALE · LONDON

© Ray Alan 2007
First published in Great Britain 2007

ISBN 978-0-7090-8393-1

Robert Hale Limited
Clerkenwell House
Clerkenwell Green
London EC1R 0HT

www.halebooks.com

The right of Ray Alan to be identified as author
of this work has been asserted by him in accordance with the
Copyright, Designs and Patents Act 1988

2 4 6 8 10 9 7 5 3 1

Typeset in 11/15pt Palatino
Printed and bound in Great Britain by
Biddles Limited, King's Lynn

CHAPTER ONE

Susie tapped her fingers against the steering wheel in frustration. Yet another traffic jam. Chelsea's evening rush should be over by now. Would she ever get to Paul's apartment? She just wanted to get this meeting out of the way before she left – and before she lost her nerve.

The lights changed to green. As she inched her way forward the photographs she'd seen in Paul's flat last night flashed unbidden before her eyes. She hadn't been able to hide her shock: pornographic pictures, practically hard-core. She shook her head as if to shake the images away.

'Look, I know you were uptight when you left here last night, but let me explain about those photographs. They were models I booked to do that special session for an overseas client,' he'd said when he phoned her that morning. 'I run a model agency, Susie, and they are just another part of my business. I would never ask *you* to take those kind of photos.' He'd then gone on to flatter her. 'You're a bloody good photographer and I like using you. You know that. You do great fashion shots of my stable but there are other kinds of pictures that pay even more. We have to live in the real world, Susie.'

'But I don't like that kind of world, Paul,' she muttered to herself now. All the same, their brief relationship had meant something to her and so she'd agreed to have dinner with him – but only to tell him face to face that it was over. He'd been most insistent he had more work for her, but her answer was going to be no. Even though he'd been very kind and lent her an expensive leather bag for her impulsive decision to take a cruise, which she'd only booked up yesterday. She was very thankful now. The timing was just right, a chance to recover from this liaison well away from everything that would remind her of him.

She glanced at her car clock as she parked opposite his block: 7.30 p.m. Not late after all. As she checked her make-up in the rear-view mirror she saw a good-looking young man come out of the building. Susie wondered if he might be one of Paul's models but then what would he be doing there on a Saturday evening? She crossed the road and rang the bell for flat six and waited, expecting to hear Paul's voice on the intercom. When there was no reply she tried again but still there was no response. As she stood there the door to the apartments opened and an elderly man came out. Before the door could close, she smiled, said, 'Thank you,' and walked past him into the building. She rang the doorbell at flat six but again there was no reply.

Annoyed, she decided to leave. She had things to do, such as finish packing. She left the building, cursing Paul Anderson.

Detective Inspector Bill Forward had spent Saturday finishing a final report on his previous case and was now looking forward to a well-earned Sunday off. He was concentrating on the crossword when the telephone rang. His wife, Jane, answered it. 'It's your new sergeant,' she told him quietly.

'Yes, sergeant?'

'Sorry to call you at home, sir. I'm in Chelsea at flat six, Albern Mansions. The cleaner found the body of a man here. His head's been badly beaten in. I phoned the doctor and he's on his way.'

'Good lad. I'll be with you as soon as I can.' Bill hung up and called to his wife. 'Sorry about this, love. I'll ring if I have to give lunch a miss.'

'How are you getting on with your new sergeant?' asked Jane.

'Early days yet, love. Marsh is young and wants to prove himself. This will be his first real case with me, so I'll soon know if we're going to get along.'

He kissed Jane on the cheek and went. After thirty years of marriage she was used to his irregular hours. She didn't complain but watched him get into his car and leave.

A police constable took Bill straight up to flat six, Albern Mansions. Detective Sergeant Marsh was carefully placing an ornamental brass golf putter into a plastic bag when Bill came in.

'Morning sir. Sorry about this.'

The inspector looked down at what had once been Paul Anderson's head. 'Not as sorry as that poor bugger, I bet.' He turned to the doctor who'd just finished examining the body. 'Morning doc. What have we got here?'

'Well, as you can see, somebody gave him a hell of a whack across the back of the head. Your sergeant has what we think to be the murder weapon. There's still a speck of blood on it despite it being wiped.'

'How long has he been dead?'

'I'll know better after the post-mortem, but anything from eleven to fourteen hours.' He walked to the door, adding, 'I should have the report with you by the morning. I'll tell my lads to collect him. Unless you want to keep him here for anything?'

'No no. Take him. I don't want my sergeant tripping over him.'

The doctor grinned and left.

'What do we know about the victim?' Bill asked next.

Sergeant Marsh put the suspected weapon down and referred to his notes. 'According to Mrs Muriel Cleave, his cleaner, Paul Anderson was in his early thirties, lived alone and ran an agency for models.'

'What sort of models?'

'The ones you see in women's magazines. There's a folder in the desk over there with photos of his clients.' He grinned, and said, 'One or two of the girls look really fit.'

'I take it you mean beautiful, not sporty? Where's Mrs Cleave now?'

'In the bedroom. The doctor gave her a sedative and she's lying down. WPC Owen is in there with her.'

Forward looked down at the body. 'Cover him over with something.'

Sergeant Marsh went to the bathroom and returned with a large bath towel which he threw over Paul Anderson's body, while Bill wandered round the room, admiring the décor.

'He had good taste, I'll say that for him.' He went through to the kitchen where he found the back door was securely bolted. Returning to the living room, he said, 'The kitchen is the only other way in to the flat I take it?'

'Yes. And there's no sign of forced entry. So the killer must have either had a key, or the victim let him or her in.'

The inspector picked up the plastic bag containing the brass golf club and studied it. 'Yes, a woman could have easily picked this up and thumped him with it.'

'I've just started to play golf,' Marsh proudly informed him.

'Have you now? And apart from the clubs and that little white ball, what's your handicap?'

'Twenty-four. I'm only a beginner of course.'

'Twenty-four, eh? Don't ever play Tiger Woods. You'll terrify him. Get that brass thing to the lab as soon as you can. Despite the blood on it, we can only assume it's the weapon at this stage. I'll go and have a word with the cleaning lady.'

Muriel Cleave was obviously still upset as Bill introduced himself. 'Detective Inspector Forward. I know you've had a nasty shock but I do need to ask you a few questions.' He gave a kindly smile.

'Yes. I understand,' she said nervously.

He sat on the edge of the bed. 'Do you usually come here on a Sunday morning?'

'Yes. I come Tuesdays, Fridays and Sundays, every week. Mr Anderson often had visitors on a Saturday night. He always likes me,' she hesitated then wiped her eyes, 'I mean *liked* me to tidy up early on Sunday mornings. Though sometimes, if they were still here, I couldn't do this bedroom. But he didn't mind as long as the rest of the place was done. I can't believe he's dead.'

'Did you ever see any of these visitors?'

She looked embarrassed as she answered, 'Once or

twice. But he was a single man, so what he did in his private life was none of my business.'

'You told my sergeant that he ran a model agency. Were any of these visitors his clients, do you know?'

'They were always pretty girls. But whether they were his models I've no idea.' She started to tremble and became tearful. 'I can't believe he's dead. Who could have done such a horrible thing?'

'That's what I intend to find out. Now, you say Mr Anderson was unmarried, but what about other relatives?'

'I know his parents are no longer alive. I've heard him mention his brother David.'

'Do you happen to know where we can contact him?'
She shook her head. 'I'm sorry.'

'It's all right. We'll find him. Before you go, leave your phone number and address with WPC Owen and she'll give you a number to contact if you think of anything else.'

As he left the bedroom a police constable called out to him. 'Excuse me, sir. The old gentleman in flat three said he saw a young woman here yesterday evening. Just before eight.'

'Did he now? Flat three you say? Right. I'll go and have a word. Meantime sergeant, see if you can get anything from the dead man's mobile and landline.'

Mr Lucas in flat three was only too pleased to assist the police. 'A terrible business, inspector. One reads about these things, but we never expect it to happen to our own neighbour.'

'No indeed, sir. Now, I'd like you to tell me anything you can about Mr Anderson.'

'Well, he was pleasant enough when we met. But not really my cup of tea you understand. Good-looking and certainly aware of it. Rather full of himself, I thought. Always had pretty girls calling on him. Ran some sort of agency I understand. Not a man I would really trust.' Giving a grin he added, 'Though I must confess, I did enjoy seeing those pretty young ladies coming and going.'

'Speaking of young ladies, the constable tells me that you saw one visiting here last night.'

'Yes. I know she was calling on Mr Anderson because I've seen them together. I was going on my regular evening walk when she hurried past me as I opened the door.'

Inspector Forward asked, 'Was she coming in, or leaving?'

'Coming in. In the past she always waited for him to let her in.'

'She didn't have a key then?'

'Apparently not.'

'What time did she call here?'

'It must have been about a quarter to eight.'

'Could you describe her?'

'Extremely good-looking and always well dressed. Blonde, and in her early twenties.'

'What length was her hair? Short, long?'

Without hesitation, the old man held his hand just below his ear. 'It came to about here.'

'Do you happen to know what car she drives?'

'It's white. But as to the make ...' He shrugged.

'Did Mr Anderson have any other visitors last night?'

'A young man came earlier. I heard him but I didn't see him. I heard him say, "It's me, Paul". It's funny how people always shout into that intercom contraption.'

'But you didn't see him?'

'I just got a glimpse of him as he entered the building. He had long hair with dreadful fair streaks in it, and it needed cutting. But I didn't really see his face. I'm sorry.'

Once he had established that Mr Lucas was unable to describe the visitor in any more detail, the inspector turned to leave.

Suddenly, Mr Lucas said, 'Wait a moment. There *was* someone else here last evening. Another young man. I saw him leave not long before the young lady arrived. And I know he was a friend of Mr Anderson's because I've seen them together. How silly of me to forget.'

'Can you describe this man?'

'Oh yes. Very good-looking. Clean-cut, well dressed, with dark hair. In his mid-twenties I think. Fancy me forgetting him. I am sorry.'

Sergeant Marsh was on his telephone in the hall when the inspector returned. He signalled that he was almost through, said, 'Thank you,' and switched off. 'I got Anderson's brother's number from his mobile address book. I left a message with his girlfriend to call us when he comes in.'

'Good. Anything else?'

'No joy from emails or phone messages but I found these.' He passed a file of photographs to the inspector. 'A bit porno for a man who's supposed to run a bona fide model agency, wouldn't you say?'

Bill Forward frowned. 'Bloody obscene. Well, if those others are bona fide his models must be earning money on the side.'

'I don't know how they can do that mixed sex stuff. Makes you sick,' said the sergeant.

Bill Forward picked up the original folder. 'I'll see if the young lady and man whom Mr Lucas saw here last evening are any of the bona fide models. I'll pop down and show him the photos.' He gave the file with the porno photos back to Marsh. 'Daren't let the old boy see those by mistake. He might get overexcited and we don't want another corpse on our hands!'

As Susie opened the door her mother looked up and gave an almost angelic smile. Susie gave her a hug and a loving kiss on the cheek. 'How are you Mum. Feeling better today?' Ruth Lewis wore a confused look that prompted Susie to give her hand a squeeze. 'It's me, Susie,' she said.

Her mother thought hard before she spoke. 'I don't think your father came today. But I'm sure he will be here soon.'

'I'm here, Mum. I've come today.' Susie smiled, trying not to show her anguish.

Suddenly, her mother showed a sign of recognition and took her daughter's hand. 'Susie.' Then she added hopefully, 'Is your father here?'

Much as she hated him being referred to as her father, she spoke kindly. 'No, darling. He couldn't get away today, but perhaps tomorrow he will.' Then Susie changed the subject. 'I've got some news for you, Mother. I'm going to have a holiday on a beautiful big cruise liner. Its name is the *Verna Castle*.'

She did her best to keep her mother's interest and gave all the details of her trip, making it sound very romantic but it was impossible to hold her attention for more than a few minutes. After an hour, Susie replaced the old flowers with new ones she'd brought, kissed her mother on the cheek and left, wondering why, if there was a God, he had ever allowed her mother to suffer this terrible illness. She took a business card from her handbag to give to the care assistant, so that she would have her mobile phone number in case she needed to make contact while she was away on her cruise. As all the staff were busy, she left the card with the girl at reception.

Trying to put all thoughts of her mother and Paul to the back of her mind, she drove to Southampton, determined to enjoy the first real holiday she had taken for ages. She felt that now her mother was settled in the Welland Nursing Home, she could spend some time away. She'd booked a last-minute berth and had had no time to tell anyone she was going.

Inspector Forward returned to the flat looking pleased with himself. He held up the photograph of a very handsome young man. 'Right, Sergeant. This man was positively iden-tified by Mr Lucas as having been seen with the victim on more than one occasion. He was also the man seen leaving the building last night. The name Julian Harper is written on the back and I want him found as soon as possible.'

'I'll get on it right away. Now, I just had an interesting chat with the victim's brother David. Seems they didn't get on. Said Paul was a reckless driver and his careless driving caused their parents' death. David has never forgiven him.'

'Interesting. And Mr Lucas is now certain that a man with blond streaks arrived around lunchtime. But if he was the killer then Harper or the girl would have found Anderson's body and called the police.'

'Well, the girl was the last one of the three to arrive, so she's number one suspect in my book.'

Inspector Forward nodded in agreement. 'It certainly looks that way. But old man Lucas didn't see her in the model file.'

CHAPTER TWO

The quayside at Southampton was a hive of activity. Susie stood on the deck of the big white liner, looking down at the crowds below as they waved farewell to their friends and relatives. Was she doing the right thing, going away for two weeks, alone? Was this really the way to get Paul out of her system and to start her life afresh?

A sudden blast from the ship's siren made her jump and she realized the *Verna Castle* was about to cast off. Then the band of the royal marines played the inevitable 'We Are Sailing' and she was caught up in the excitement as cameras clicked and hundreds of paper streamers were thrown over the side of the ship.

As the ship moved slowly from the quay, she knew that it was too late to change her mind. She was heading for the open sea and the holiday she dreamed of had really begun.

At the same time Erik de Jager received a phone call at his luxury home in Cobham, Surrey, from his paid informant at the Chelsea police station.

'I have some news for you. Don't worry, I'm using a public phone.'

'Good. So what's the news?'

'Paul Anderson was found dead in his apartment this morning. Somebody killed him. A blow to the head.'

'Good God!' de Jager was unable to conceal the panic in his voice. 'Do they know who did it?'

'They're looking for a young man and a woman. That's all I know at the moment. I'll be in touch as soon as I hear something definite, but I thought you'd want to know he was dead.'

'Yes. Yes. You did right. Keep in touch but be careful.' De Jager hung up and went to his cocktail cabinet. After pouring himself a whisky, he sat at his desk, trying to take in the news he had just received.

Officially he was in the property business, but he also dealt in drugs and he bought people too when he needed them. After meeting Paul at a dinner, and learning about the way his models travelled to Europe and further afield, he cultivated the young man. It wasn't difficult to persuade Paul to become part of his distribution network. He had spotted someone as greedy as himself, who didn't care what route he took to acquire his wealth.

'Believe me, my friend, the risk to us is nil,' de Jager had told him with confidence. 'The innocent courier is never aware of what they are carrying or who plants it on them, and so, they are never able to name anyone … Foolproof, you see. And once my associate relieves them of it at its final destination, voilà!' He threw his arms up in triumph.

De Jager had last seen Paul a few days ago when they had dinner together at the Carlton Hotel. Paul brought Susie Cunningham to the dinner.

During the meal he learned all about her photographic work, her mother and the cruise she had suddenly decided to take. He was particularly interested when she mentioned that the ship was to call at Piraeus, the port for Athens.

Now, here he was, learning that his lucrative association with Paul was at an end. But something else gave him cause for concern. Had Paul given her the leather bag? Had he concealed the package from her? Or was it still at the dead man's apartment?

The cabin was not as big as the brochure had suggested but it was comfortable. It had cost a little extra to have it to herself but Susie felt it was worth it to have her own bathroom.

She finished unpacking the big leather bag that Paul had insisted she took, but it was too big to go under her bed. As she was wondering what to do, there was a knock on her door. 'Good morning, madam. My name is Heather and I'm your cabin stewardess. If there is anything you want during the cruise just push the bell and either myself or Heidi will be pleased to help you.'

Susie smiled. 'Thanks. In fact this bag won't go under my bed. Anything you can do?'

'I can take it to the baggage room. It'll be safe there.'

'Oh, thank you.'

'What about the other one?'

'I think the pink one will go under OK. I'll finish unpacking it and see. If it won't go I'll ring you.'

Erik de Jager had been anxiously waiting for a call from his police informant. When it came he answered immediately.

'De Jager ...Yes? ...They found nothing. Nothing at all?

... You're sure? ... Excellent ... Keep in touch.' He hung up and poured himself another large whisky. He now knew that the unsuspecting Susie Cunningham *had* taken the package with her. The package his associate on board would soon be able to retrieve. His scheme appeared to be going as planned and he was pleased with himself, and the fact that his generous payments to a police filing clerk were paying off.

When Susie entered the dining room she was shown to a table for six. An elderly couple were already there. As Susie was wondering where to sit, a good-looking man arrived and made the decision for her. 'Good evening.' He smiled. 'Why don't you sit here? Then you two roses can be separated by a thorn.' She was so taken aback, Susie did as he suggested and sat to his left, which put him between herself and the wife of the elderly couple, who introduced themselves as the Reverend Lionel Weston and his wife Sybil. He introduced himself as James Kerr and Sybil was obviously delighted to have the young man next to her.

Susie guessed that he was in his thirties and thought him a bit too confident. As he began making conversation on the joys of cruising, an attractive young woman was escorted to the table by the restaurant manager. Her beautiful dark hair made a perfect frame for her lovely face, and her dress fitted snugly on a neat figure that any woman would envy.

Her arrival stopped James in his tracks. He rose to his feet, which prompted the reverend to do the same. Both men stood as the restaurant manager drew back a chair for her. As she sat, he quickly cleared the cutlery, napkin, glasses and chair from the sixth place, converting it to a table for five, as if by magic.

The new arrival gave a warm, alluring smile and said, in a self-assured voice, her dark eyes sparkling, 'Good evening. I'm Carol Mason.'

As they all introduced themselves, Susie was amused at the way James instantly switched his attention from her to Carol Mason, who was now sitting between Susie and the Reverend Weston.

'Well, reverend, I bet you had no idea when you booked that you would be sitting at a table surrounded by beauty queens, eh?' James said with a grin.

Sybil was quick to answer. 'I don't think Lionel has ever thought of me as a beauty queen, Mr Kerr.'

'Come now Mrs Weston.' James flattered her.

'Call me Sybil, please.' She smiled.

'Sybil it is. And I'm James.' He turned to Carol. 'And do I call you Miss Mason or Carol?' Then quickly added, 'Or is it Mrs Mason perhaps?'

'Actually it's ms,' she said with a false smile.

'Really? I can never understand why attractive women want to keep their marital status a secret,' James replied.

'But you aren't an attractive woman,' Carol retorted. Then quickly turning to Susie, she said, 'But you are, Susie. I always wanted to be a genuine blonde.'

Taken aback, Susie said, 'Thanks.'

Smiling enviously, Sybil said, 'I could never look like you lovely young ladies, I'm afraid. Now, let's have a look at the menu, shall we? The beef sounds delicious.' She went on, 'I shall have melon, then beef. And if I've got room I might be very naughty and have cherries and ice cream.'

'Oh, I think I'll definitely have a yummy desert,' said Carol. 'You too, Susie?'

Susie smiled to herself as the waiter came for their orders. She guessed she was going to like Carol.

Bill and Jane Forward had not quite finished their supper when the police surgeon called. 'Sorry to bother you at home like this but, although you will have my report in the morning, I thought you might be interested to know what I found.'

'Go on.'

'Well, time of death, as near as I can be certain, between seven and nine yesterday evening. Cause of death, at least two extremely vicious blows to the head, and the lab has confirmed it was the brass golf club. But there was something else I think you'll be interested to hear.'

'What's that?'

'During the last hour of his life, the victim had sexual intercourse with someone.'

'Maybe his young blonde visitor. Nothing unusual about that is there?'

'No. But at sometime during that same period, someone had sexual intercourse with *him*.'

Bill Forward was surprised. 'Did they now? Anything else?'

'No. The rest is in my report. I knew you were anxious for my findings, hence this call.'

'Thank you, doctor. I appreciate it. Goodnight to you.' He hung up and was deep in thought when his wife called.

'Are you coming to finish your supper, Bill?'

*

'I couldn't eat another thing.' Sybil patted her stomach and smiled as she dabbed her mouth with her napkin. Turning to her husband she instructed, 'And you've had enough, dear. Must watch our figures.' Then, turning to the others, giggled, 'What's left of them.'

Reverend Weston put down his cutlery in obedience and gave a half-hearted smile.

Sybil rose from her seat and addressing her husband, said, 'Come along, dear. We still have some unpacking to do. Then we'll have an early night.' She smiled at the others. 'You will forgive us, won't you? Enjoy the rest of the evening. Come on, Lionel.'

He rose and nodded to the others as he took his wife by the arm and escorted her from the table.

When the Westons had retired James asked Susie and Carol for a drink, but Carol quickly declined for both the girls, leaving a disgruntled James staring after them. She led the way to what she promised was: 'A real find. It's a little tucked-away bar, where the lights aren't too bright. I hope the same gorgeous young bartender is on again!'

Carol insisted on getting the first round and returned to their table with two Martini cocktails. 'Here you are. Wait till you taste that.'

Susie agreed that her drink was perfect and the two girls began chatting. Susie told Carol about her job as a free-lance photographer. When she mentioned shooting models, Carol screwed up her face. 'There are one or two that want properly shooting. How some can command those bloody enormous fees for looking like living corpses, I will never know. Sorry.'

Susie smiled. 'No need to be. I agree. Some of them even

make me feel uncomfortable. But that's the way some people want them, I'm afraid.'

As Susie finished talking about her work, Carol asked the inevitable question. 'And what about your love life? I take it you aren't one of the trapped or you wouldn't be here alone?'

'No, I'm not one of the "trapped", as you put it. Had one or two boyfriends but no one person in particular.'

'Only one or two? With your looks I would have thought you'd be beating them off like flies.'

'I wish! What about you, Carol. What do you do?'

'As little as possible. My dad's well off and allows me to do anything I want. Within reason that is. I have no horrible brothers or sisters to share my daddy with and so, you are looking at a very happy girl.'

'A very lucky one too. My father died when I was young so I never knew what he was really like. Is your mum still alive?'

'Oh yes, very much alive and on the committee of every charity in the county, and anything else she can be talked into. And in case you were going to ask, she spoils me as much as my father does. Where do you live, Susie?'

'I have a flat in Wimbledon. What about you?'

'Oh, I have a place in London but spend a lot of time with my parents in Albury.'

'Albury? Where's that?'

'Between Dorking and Guildford.' Then putting on a posh voice, said, 'Surrey actually, old thing.'

'Ah. The stockbroker belt, eh? So daddy's *really* rich.'

Carol laughed, then began to yawn. 'Excuse me! I'm knackered. Would you mind very much if we call it a night?'

23

'Of course not. I still have some unpacking to do.'

'OK, see you at breakfast then,' said Carol. 'Ciao. Sleep well.'

When Susie reached her cabin she found a note pushed under her door. It read:

Please forgive me for behaving so badly at dinner. I'm afraid you must think me quite awful.

Please let me prove that I'm not. May I buy you a drink before lunch tomorrow?

I shall not be in the dining room for breakfast but would very much like to meet you in the Neptune bar at about 12 noon.

My cabin number is C24. Ring me!

James.

She sat for a moment. Why not go and have a drink with him? After all, he'd taken the trouble to write and apologize for his behaviour. Not an easy thing to do, she thought. Besides, what harm would there be? It was too late to ring now. She decided to finish her unpacking as she had intended, and call James in the morning.

When Sergeant Marsh arrived at the station the next day, Inspector Forward was already at his desk.

'Morning, sir. You're early.'

'No, sunshine. You're late! Here's the doctor's report. I think you'll find it interesting reading. We need to find Julian Harper and the blonde asap. And I want to know who the man with blonde streaks is too. I think we should check with the other residents in case it was one of them he was visiting.'

Sergeant Marsh looked confused. 'I thought old Mr Lucas heard him say he was visiting Paul Anderson.'

'No. What he heard was the man speak into the intercom and say, "It's me Paul."'

'Well, there you are, guv.'

'But suppose his name was Paul and he was ringing another apartment? He would have said, "It's me. Paul," wouldn't he? Check it anyway. Then if I'm right we can eliminate him.'

'OK. I'll get over there and see if anyone knows who he is. And I think I've got a lead on our blonde lady. With a bit of luck this could be the one we're looking for.'

The Inspector looked up from his desk with surprise. 'Well? Come on, sergeant. Don't keep it a secret.'

'I began phoning models on Anderson's books. I've only got a reply from two, but when I described the blonde we were interested in tracing, they both said she sounded like the photographer who did their last photo session. Susie Cunningham.'

'Any address?'

'No. But her phone number was in the victim's address book. I tried it a couple of times but it was on answer-phone. It's a Wimbledon area code. I was going to look it up, first thing this morning. And by the way, there was no Julian Harper among the numbers in the victim's—'

'I wish you'd stop calling him the victim. I know Harper isn't listed because I checked. Now get cracking and find our mystery blonde, will you? But before you do that can you organize a large mug of black coffee?' he said, with a kindly smile.

'I'll get one of the PCs on it right away.'

As Sergeant Marsh left the office, Bill Forward sat back

and closed his eyes, deep in thought. Was the killer the male model as the post-mortem findings would suggest? Or was it the blonde? His gut feeling told him that it wasn't that simple and he sat going over everything in his mind. Then another thought came to him. How long would he have to wait for his coffee?

Susie had only the Westons for company at breakfast, and when she returned to her cabin, she tried phoning James, but there was no reply. Just as she was wondering what to do with her morning the telephone rang. It was Carol.

'Hi, Carol. Chickened out of breakfast then?'

'Truth is, I had a bloody awful night. After I left you I really was going to bed. Then a gorgeous officer asked me to have a drink with him. How could I refuse?'

Susie was smiling to herself as she asked, 'What happened?'

'Oh, nothing like that, Susie. Just that the one drink became three. Or was it four? Anyway I woke up looking terrible and simply couldn't show my face. Not when I saw it in the mirror. Yuk.'

Susie laughed. 'You couldn't have looked that bad. Anyway, I had a very nice, quiet breakfast with the Westons. They really are quite sweet when you get to know them.'

'So where was James?' Carol asked.

'He didn't show. I don't think he was too keen on facing you to tell the truth.'

Carol chuckled. 'Is he really that scared of me?'

'I think you could say that. He put a note under my door last night.'

'He didn't!'

'Asking me for a drink before lunch.'

'Well, well. He was rude to me but apologizes to *you*. I think you should watch him, darling. He could be trying to get your knickers off.'

'Don't be ridiculous. I think he's just trying to make up for his behaviour. Anyway. I'll find out at noon and let you know after lunch.'

CHAPTER THREE

Sergeant Marsh was impressed by Susie Cunningham's home in Wimbledon. Daneham Court was an impressive block of flats that had a porter's lodge at the entrance of the drive. Marsh parked the car and they went to the block leading to flat number four. Forward pressed the door entry and as he waited the porter approached them.

'Can I be of assistance, gentlemen?'

Showing his warrant card, the inspector introduced himself. 'Detective Inspector Forward, and this is Sergeant Marsh, Chelsea CID.'

The porter was both impressed and intrigued. 'How can I be of help, gentlemen?'

'We are interested in the whereabouts of a young lady we understand lives at number four.'

'Oh, that would be Miss Cunningham. She isn't there though. She told me she was going on holiday and would be back in two weeks.'

The inspector was surprised. 'When was this?'

'Yesterday morning. When I helped carry her bags to her car.'

'Did she say where she was going?' asked the sergeant.

'Not on her holiday, no. But I do know that she was

going to see her mother on the way. Poor woman's in a nursing home and likely to be in there for some time, so I understand.'

Bill Forward was not hopeful when he asked, 'Do you happen to know where this nursing home is?'

'It's in Haslemere somewhere. I've got a name and a phone number in the office. If you'd like to follow me, gentlemen....' As they walked to his office, the porter continued, 'She wrote down all the details the last time she went to see her mother. Said she was expecting a phone call from a gentleman that she was hoping to do some work for.' He looked through his paper work, then suddenly, 'Ah. Here it is: "If a Paul Anderson should call tell him I'm at the Welland Nursing Home, Haslemere." That's where her mother is, inspector.'

Even after learning that Susie's mother, Ruth Lewis, was suffering from Alzheimers, the inspector decided to try and talk to her.

He was greeted by the nursing home's manager, who introduced him to Ruth's primary carer. She led the way to Ruth's bright little room. 'The old lady has good days and bad ones. Sometimes she gets a bit agitated, but she's well enough in herself.'

'Ruth Lewis – she uses her second husband's surname. Her daughter keeps her real father's name?' Forward mused as they went in.

'That's right. Though we haven't seen much of Mr Lewis lately.' She raised her voice. 'Ruth, dear. This gentleman has come to visit you. He's a friend of your Susie. Isn't that a nice surprise?'

Ruth stared at the inspector with a puzzled expression. 'Are you Paul?' she asked. 'Is Susie with you?'

'No, Mrs Lewis. I'm not Paul. My name is Bill and I need to know where Susie is. Can you help me?'

Ruth stared back to the window and then said, 'Susie went away.'

'Did she tell you where she was going?' He knew that it was probably a wasted question but hoped for a positive reply.

Ruth Lewis closed her eyes and concentrated. After a while she turned and said, 'Susie's gone to the castle.'

'Did she say which castle she was going to?'

Ruth looked at the inspector. Then, obviously confused, she asked, 'Are you a new doctor? I don't want to see any more doctors.' Tears started to fill her eyes and her carer put her arm around her.

'This gentleman isn't a doctor, Ruth. He's trying to find Susie and hoped that you could tell him where she is. Just now you mentioned a castle. Remember?'

There was a long pause while Ruth tried to think. 'Castle? Her friend will know.' She sounded confident.

Bill Forward took over again. 'What's her friend's name? Can you remember that, Mrs Lewis?'

'If my husband comes, we'll have tea together today.' Ruth looked through the window. 'The garden would be nice.'

The carer gave the inspector a shrug of despair and signalled that they should leave. Forward nodded then turned to Ruth Lewis and smiled. 'It was nice to meet you, Mrs Lewis. Thank you for letting me come and see you.'

As they were about to leave, Ruth Lewis said, 'I had a friend called Verna.' Trying hard to concentrate she added, 'Not Castle though. I think it was Saunders.'

The inspector stopped and went back to Ruth Lewis. 'Verna Castle? Is that who Susie has gone away with?'

Ruth ignored his question and said, 'I always liked tea in the garden.' Then turned to him. 'But no pills. Promise they won't give me more pills?'

The inspector patted her hand and smiled. 'I promise.' He and the carer left the room and walked downstairs.

'I did warn, you inspector. Sorry, but this is one of her good days.'

'Has she ever mentioned this Verna woman before?'

'Not that I can remember. Mind you, I'm not with her all the time. I can ask the night-time carer. She spends more time with her than anyone else.'

'If you wouldn't mind. I would appreciate it.' He was about to leave and then stopped. 'By the way. Has she got a photo of Susie, do you know?'

She became thoughtful for a moment. 'Now that you mention it, no.'

'Thank you again for your time.' Giving her a smile he left the nursing home.

Sergeant Marsh was waiting by the car. 'Any luck, guv?'

'Wasted journey,' he said, shaking his head as he got into the car. Then, as the sergeant got in he added, 'Well, almost.'

'How do you mean …' He started the car. 'Almost?'

'Poor woman doesn't really know what's going on. However, she did say a name, Verna Castle, and her carer told me this was a new name she'd started mentioning. Whether it's someone her daughter went away with or someone she just thought of from the old days, God knows. We'll check it out anyway.'

'Starting with me going through all the Castles in the phone book, I suppose?' Sergeant Marsh groaned.

'And while you're doing that, I'll see how many Castles of Britain are named Verna.'

'That will take all of ten minutes,' said the sergeant sarcastically.

'Just think. When you're an inspector you'll have a happy sergeant to do all your nasty jobs for you. Drive carefully, I'll look out for a pub and buy you a nice ploughman's and a glass of shandy.'

'Shandy?'

'I don't want you drinking and driving, do I? It happens to be against the law. Now there's a nice looking place. I bet they serve a lovely shandy in there.' He watched with amusement his sergeant sulking as they pulled into the car park.

Susie abandoned her intention to explore the ship as soon as she saw the size of the shopping area. It was far bigger than she could ever have imagined. By the time she had looked at all the clothes she couldn't afford, and tested different shades of lipstick and perfume that she had no intention of buying, it was gone 11.30. Susie was checking her watch when she sensed that someone was watching her. She looked up and saw a man quickly avert his eyes from her direction and appear to show interest in a bottle of perfume. He obviously had no intention of actually buying anything and left the shop. Despite his air of innocence, Susie was convinced that he had been staring at her and she felt uncomfortable. The man was a passenger in his fifties she guessed, and there was something about him that Susie didn't like. She hurried back to her cabin, taking the wrong turning in her agitation.

She arrived at B deck and realized that her cabin was at the other end of the corridor, and that she should have taken the forward stairway. As she was approaching her cabin, James Kerr appeared at the foot of the aft stairway which surprised her.

'Hello. I thought you were on C deck,' she said.

'I was coming to see you,' said James awkwardly. 'I wondered if perhaps I'd left a note at the wrong cabin.'

'Oh no, I got your note. In fact I tried to ring you but I got no reply.'

'Sorry. I must have been in the shower.' Then hopefully he asked, 'Will you have that drink with me?'

She gave a friendly smile. 'Give me ten minutes.'

James returned her smile. 'Yes, of course. See you in the Neptune bar.'

Erik de Jager was in his office working on a new property deal when his private telephone rang. There was only one person he was hoping to hear from. He answered and wasn't disappointed.

'I thought you'd like to know that our friend has paid a visit to a certain lady at Haslemere and the name of Verna Castle was mentioned.' The informant awaited the reaction.

'Damn! This could prove a problem. I had hoped that our young lady's whereabouts would not be known so soon.'

The caller enjoyed being able to tease his benefactor. 'I don't think you need worry. He's convinced the name belongs to a friend of your young lady and that they are on holiday together. He's desperately trying to find an address for the mysterious Miss Castle.'

'You're positive he has no idea as to the identity of our Miss Castle?'

'I tell you he is pulling out all the stops going through telephone directories and has even got someone checking the registry of voters.'

'I can't afford to take chances. I'll contact my friend on board and have him retrieve my property as soon as he thinks it prudent to do so. Anything else?'

'Not at the moment.'

'Good work. Keep in touch and be careful. I don't want you jeopardizing your position there.'

'You can rely on me. I really must go. I took an early lunch so that I could phone you. Better get to the canteen or they might think it funny that I'm not actually eating.'

After he'd rung off, Erik de Jager thought it was time to make another call. He looked up the Inmarsat number that was required to call vessels at sea.

James Kerr had already finished one vodka and tonic by the time Susie arrived at the Neptune bar.

'You look great!' he said, moving aside so she could sit down. His voice sounded warm and sincere which made her feel that he was genuine.

'Thanks.'

'What will you have?'

'Campari and soda please.'

As they chatted about the ship and their fellow passengers, the atmosphere became more relaxed and Susie decided to change the subject. 'What sort of work do you do. Anything exciting?'

He looked around the bar furtively, then quietly said, 'If I said that I worked for MI5, would you believe me?'

In a whisper she replied, 'Not even if you produced your James Bond ID card.' Susie was beginning to enjoy his company.

'How very wise,' said James. 'Never trust a secret agent.'

She liked the smile he gave her and he seemed like a really nice person. His cockiness had disappeared and was replaced by a warmer personality.

'Seriously. What sort of work do you do?' she asked.

'I'm a mortician,' James replied.

'You're joking!' she said, hoping he was.

He chuckled. 'The conversation always goes a bit quiet when I tell anyone what I do.'

'But you don't look like an undertaker.'

'What are we supposed to look like?' His smile broadened. 'People say that about murderers. Yet nobody can describe what one actually looks like. Can you?'

She gave an incredulous look. 'It's just that you look so ordinary. I mean, I can't imagine you dealing with ... Oh, let's talk about something else.'

James laughed quietly to himself. 'Certainly. I'd rather we talked about you anyway. What do you do to earn a crumb?'

His question amused her. 'I'm a freelance photographer. Which really means that there wasn't a company that wanted to employ a woman with a Nikon camera, so I work for myself.'

'Good for you. What sort of work do you do?'

'Anything from weddings to ...' she noticed his eyebrow lift in a mischievous manner and said quickly, 'You don't have to look at me like that, Mr Kerr. I wouldn't even dream of getting involved in your business.' She was finding James much more likeable now. 'I was going to say, anything from weddings to location shots for brochures and magazines. As a matter of fact, I recently took photographs of some things I think you would have liked very much.'

'Such as?'

'Beautiful, gorgeous, female models.' She laughed as he pretended disinterest.

'I'd like to see some of your work, I bet you're good. Have you got any with you?' James asked.

'No. Why would I bring samples of my work on holiday?'

James was positive in his reply. 'So that people can see them of course. Someone has to do the photographs for these cruise brochures. Someone has to sell their work to the cruise line. So why not you?'

His comment made sense. The thought had never entered her head. Even when she browsed the brochure before booking the cruise, she hadn't looked at the photographs in any way as potential business. And that annoyed her. Here was an undertaker, teaching her how to think like a real professional photographer. 'My dear James, you are absolutely right. Thank you. Finish your drink. The next round is on me.'

They talked cameras till Susie suddenly realized it was time to meet Carol for lunch, and she suggested they both go and meet her.

Lunch proved uneventful. The Weston's were first to finish and leave the table. Then Carol got up from her chair and asked Susie, 'When shall we have our get together?'

'Any time that suits you. I've nothing planned.'

'What about the Queen's lounge. Say, in an hour?'

'Fine.'

When Carol had gone, James asked, 'What have you planned to do when we get to Lisbon?'

'Nothing in particular. I wondered whether to book on one of the half-day tours. Why do you ask?'

'Well, it's just a thought but if you've never been before, I would suggest that you look round the town in the morning, and see Sintra after that. Perhaps have lunch there, before visiting the palace.'

'Palace?'

'Oh, you must see that.' James insisted. 'It started life as a monastery. Then a Bavarian prince added to it in fifteen hundred and something, and it was converted into a palace. I really do recommend you see it. It looks like something out of a Walt Disney film. Really stunning.'

Susie had a feeling she knew what was coming as she said, 'Really?'

'Oh yes. The original monastery section is covered from floor to ceiling in beautiful tiles. Look, I shall be going there myself. Why don't we go together? If you want to of course.' He waited expectantly for her answer.

Susie thought for a moment. 'It sounds too good an offer to refuse, I'd love to. That's the day after tomorrow, isn't it?'

'Yes. We're there until ten at night, so we've plenty of time to do everything.'

They hadn't realized that the dining room was almost empty and tables were being cleared.

As they walked out together James put his hand on her waist, as if guiding her. It was a bit early in the cruise for that sort of thing, she thought. Then, just as she was beginning to realize how nice his hand felt against her, he removed it.

'I must go to the radio room and send a fax,' he told her. 'Perhaps we could meet later for a drink?'

'Oh, yes. Give me a ring. Or shall we meet in that quiet bar again?' she suggested.

'That would be nice,' he said. 'I'll ring you later and arrange what time to meet. OK?'

'OK.' She smiled.

Susie went to her cabin, and as she walked in, had an eerie feeling that someone had been there, touching her things. Her toiletries and make-up tray had been moved. And her empty suitcase was protruding slightly from under the bed. Looking around the cabin, everything else seemed to be as she had left it. But the thought of somebody breaking in like a burglar became preposterous and she convinced herself that Heather the stewardess had simply moved her things when she was cleaning the cabin and making the bed.

Erik de Jager wasn't pleased when his associate on the *Verna Castle* informed him that he hadn't been able to find the package. 'But don't worry. Tonight is the captain's welcome aboard cocktail party, so everyone will be there. As soon as I feel it's safe, I shall slip away and leave her a complimentary drink to prepare for my visit later.'

'I hope you know what you're doing.'

'Trust me. The package should be with me tonight.'

'As soon as you have it, let me know. But be careful. Be very careful,' de Jager instructed him. 'Just make certain that it's safe. And the next time we speak, we must refer to the item as a gift. Just in case we are overheard.'

'Of course.'

As de Jager hung up, he was praying that his associate was right and would have no more trouble in retrieving the package.

Susie arrived at the Queen's lounge first. She watched as Carol made her 'entrance' and as Carol got nearer, Susie thought what an attractive woman she was and wondered why she hadn't got herself a nice millionaire with a yacht and a villa in the south of France. There was a lot more to the flamboyant and beautiful Carol, of that she was certain, and during their chat she hoped to learn what it was.

'Darling. You look wonderful. How the hell can you look so bloody marvellous with hardly a sign of make-up?' Carol sat and smiled. 'I hate you.'

'Oh, come on, Carol. You have looks any woman would kill for. You know that.'

An impish grin appeared. 'I know. But I do have to rely a lot on Clinique.' She sighed. 'Enough about my terribly sad life. What shall we have to drink?' They ordered two cocktails, then Carol asked, 'Tell me, what made you come away on your own? Was it some bastard of a man?' Carol eagerly awaited the reply.

Susie paused before answering. 'In a way, I suppose. But not entirely. I just needed to get away. I'd finished a rather long session, shooting a load of studio stuff and what with one thing and another, decided a cruise would be nice. Get right away from everything for a while and go home feeling like starting afresh. What about you? I bet you've had your share of men problems.'

Carol laughed. 'It's the other way round actually. The

men have had problems with me! Sometimes I think, poor sods. Then other times I think, up theirs!' She gave a loud hearty laugh. Then quickly cupped her hand over her mouth as some of the sleeping passengers woke with a start.

'You really are a one-off aren't you?' Susie said quietly.

'If you think that, darling, then you've led a very boring, sheltered life.'

Susie laughed. 'Well, when I'm with you I think I must have done. Now, can I ask you a serious question?'

Carol settled back in her chair. 'Shoot. As you pretty photographers say.'

'Well, you told me earlier about not having to work, and I know you're spoilt rotten by your father and probably need never have to worry about material things again, but ...'

'But what about a personal relationship? Why haven't I got a fantastic husband?'

'Well. Yes. I mean, you're an extremely attractive woman, so why are you alone?'

The question caused Carol to consider for a moment before answering, 'Perhaps it's because I've never really met anyone I wanted to be with for the rest of my life. There have been a number of men I've wanted to jump into bed with but I—'

'I wasn't meaning someone for purely sex,' Susie cut in. 'I meant someone to be happy with when you aren't having sex with them.'

'To be perfectly honest. I haven't met that man yet. Now can we change the subject? There's a question I need to ask. If you don't mind, that is?'

'Of course not,' said Susie.

'What are you wearing for the captain's cocktail party? I don't want us to clash.'

'Well, it's a toss-up between a long black number or a knee-length blue creation.'

'Go for the blue and show a bit of leg. To be honest, I'm surprised the weather is going to be smooth enough to have the party tonight. The Bay of Biscay can be bloody rough sometimes. So we're lucky.'

'Yes. I suppose we are.'

'Do you mind if I ask another question?' Carol asked.

Susie wondered what was coming. 'No. I don't mind.'

Carol whispered, 'Where are those bloody drinks?'

Unable to hide her amusement, Susie realized she should stop trying to be serious with Carol. As the drinks arrived, she decided to just enjoy the outrageous personality that was the only Carol Mason she was likely to see during the cruise. Even so, she felt there was an interesting, even kind person behind that flamboyant façade.

Bill Forward had a light snack at the canteen, then went to see his superintendent. 'Hello, sir. Have you got a minute?'

Superintendent Lamb looked up from the paperwork on his desk. 'Come in, Forward. How's the case coming along?'

'I want to put out an all ports warning for two people wanted for questioning in our murder inquiry, sir.'

'Right.' He took a form from his desk. 'And they are?'

'One, a female, Susie Cunningham. Blonde, early twenties.' Bill Forward waited for him to finish writing.

'And who's the second?'

'Julian Harper. Dark hair, also early twenties. We should

have a photograph later today. And could you make it priority sir?'

'I will. These are the two seen by your eyewitness I take it?'

'Yes. Unfortunately they both seem to have disappeared. I don't want them leaving the country.'

'Consider it done.'

'Thank you, sir.'

The sun had broken through and although it was still cool on deck, the sky was clear and visibility good for getting some pictures, Susie decided. It was then that she noticed the man who had stared at her in the perfume shop. Although he appeared to be engrossed in a book, Susie had a scary feeling that she was being observed by him. Her suspicion was confirmed when she pointed her camera in his direction and he concealed his face behind the book. She turned away from him, wondering why he appeared interested in her. Perhaps it was just her imagination, she thought. Even so, he made her feel very uncomfortable and she decided to leave the deck.

After he had been to the radio room, James went to the indoor pool. It was quiet at this time of day and he needed time to think. He had the pool almost to himself and his thoughts turned to his table companions. Carol, the dark-haired beauty, and in particular Susie. With honey-blonde hair and a Scandinavian complexion, she was a girl who would never let you down in company. Unlike sexually alluring Carol would. Susie had a natural charm that any man would fall for. Now here he was, the bachelor, who swore that no woman would ever get under his skin again and make a fool of him, beginning to feel completely comfortable in the company of a woman who was in fact, still a complete stranger. After a few lengths of the pool, he got out and sat on a sun lounger. Before he met Susie again, he wanted to get things straightened out in his mind, as she was starting to create a problem for him.

Susie was walking towards the lift when a young man came up behind her. 'Excuse me,' he said. 'Aren't you a photographer?' As she turned to see who was addressing her, she saw an extremely handsome young man in his mid-twenties.

'Er, yes. Yes I am,' Susie replied.

'I thought so.' He smiled. 'I saw you on the deck with your camera, and it suddenly clicked.'

'Camera's usually do,' Said Susie with a smile.

The young man laughed. 'There was no pun intended. It's just that I did some modelling for a knitwear company last year and you did the photo session. My name's Mark by the way. Mark Sutherland.'

'Oh yes, I remember now,' said Susie. 'Decided to spend your ill-gotten gains on a cruise, have you?' she joked.

'Not quite. I've got a modelling assignment in Athens, so I shall be getting off in Piraeus.'

'Lucky you. Combining work with pleasure, eh?' Suddenly the lift arrived and Susie stepped in. 'Nice to see you again, Mark. See you later no doubt.'

'I hope so,' he said.

The lift doors closed, leaving Susie wondering why he was travelling to an assignment by sea, when all the models she knew normally went by air. As she went to her cabin, she considered what a strange coincidence it was that they should both be travelling on the same ship together.

CHAPTER FOUR

Bill Forward showed his search warrant to the porter and explained the reason for returning to Susie Cunningham's apartment. The porter opened the door and led the inspector to the living room.

'I know there's one here of Miss Cunningham and her mother.' Taking a framed photograph from the sideboard, he said, 'Yes. Here it is.'

Bill Forward took the photograph and recognized Ruth Lewis immediately. The attractive young blonde with her was just as Mr Lucas had described. 'She certainly is a lovely looking young lady. And it's a fairly recent photo judging by her mother's appearance.'

'It was taken soon after her mother went into the nursing home, I believe,' said the porter.

'I shall take this and see that it's returned as soon as we have a copy. And while I'm here I'll have a look and see if there's anything to tell us where Miss Cunningham has gone on this holiday of hers.' He looked at the porter who was hovering behind him. 'You don't have to wait. I'll give you a shout when I'm finished here.'

'Yes. Yes, right. If you don't need me ...' Reluctantly, the porter left Forward on his own to search the flat at his leisure. Despite carefully examining her papers and her mail, there was nothing to give the slightest hint as to where Susie had gone, which he found very odd. It seemed she had disappeared on a whim – or had someone arranged for her to disappear?

After leaving the apartment, he went straight to old Mr Lucas who confirmed that the girl in the photograph and the girl he'd seen on Saturday evening were one and the same.

He returned to his office and scanned Susie's photograph into the PC and had it sent out nationally, and to all air and sea ports. He was convinced that someone, somewhere, must know of Susie Cunningham's whereabouts. He just wished he could make some progress with the name Verna Castle.

After the gruelling task of identifying his brother, David Anderson arrived home to find his girlfriend, Lisa, curled up in an armchair, reading the paper and smoking a cigarette. When she heard him come in she quickly threw the cigarette into the inglenook fireplace and waved the newspaper about to try and remove any trace of smoke.

'Hello, sweetie. Didn't expect you back so early.'

He waved his hand in front of his nose. 'I can tell. Phew. You've been puffing the dreaded weed again and I asked you not to. Not in the house. It stinks the place out.'

'Sorry. Can I get you anything?'

'No, I had a drink on the train.' He sat in the other armchair.

'Was it awful?' she asked with concern.

'Not very nice. I don't know how the hell they did it but they made him look as though he was just asleep. It was really weird. I almost expected him to open his eyes,' he said with a shudder.

Lisa screwed her nose up in disgust. 'Sounds horrible. What else did the police say?'

'Oh, they asked if I had ever heard of certain people.' He took a piece of paper from his pocket and studied it, then screwed it up and threw it into the bin.

'What was that?' she asked.

'Just some names of people the police are looking for. I've never heard of any of them, so I wasn't much help.'

Curious, she retrieved the paper from the bin and straightened it out to read the names to herself.

David was amused and said jokingly, 'I bet you know everyone on that list, don't you?'

She shook her head. 'Not the first two. But I think the third one is what my cousin went on.'

'What are you talking about, went on?'

'*Verna Castle*. I'm sure that was the name of it.'

'Name of what?'

'The ship my cousin went on last summer. Yes, I'm right. It was definitely the *Verna Castle*. I remember him talking about it.'

'So it's a ship! Not a person. You're certain of that?'

'Yeah, definitely.'

David suddenly became very thoughtful. After a few moments he asked Lisa if she would mind going back to her own flat as he wanted to be alone and do some work. She'd stayed three nights in a row and he was feeling the need for some space.

After she had left, he recalled what Inspector Forward had said about the suspect, Susie Cunningham, having gone away with her friend 'Verna'. David was now intrigued as to what this Cunningham girl had to do with his brother's death. And if she'd killed him, why?

David tossed various thoughts around in his head and began to conceive a plan of action. Why not try and join the ship at one of its ports of call? Get to know Susie Cunningham and, without telling her who he was, possibly end up with an exclusive story from a woman who had committed murder. Not just any murder. His brother's! He knew that such a story could earn him a small fortune. But then another thought quelled his enthusiasm. He would have to tell the inspector of his discovery. Or would he? He needed to consider the situation very carefully before rushing into anything. He poured himself a drink and tried to relax as he gave the matter serious thought.

Susie was asleep in her cabin when the phone rang, and still not properly awake as she reached out to pick up the receiver. 'Hello?' she said, her voice slightly croaky.

'Sorry. Did I wake you?' James asked.

'I must have dozed off.' As she looked at her watch, Susie said with a start, 'Gosh, is that the time?'

'I make it nearly six o'clock. It's the sea air getting to you,' said James.

She cleared her throat. 'I can't believe it. I thought I'd have a rest and here it is getting on for dinner time! It must have been that drink that knocked me out,' She said, shaking her head to try and clear it. 'I was dead to the world when you rang.'

'What drink was that?'

'The complimentary welcome-aboard drink. Didn't you get one?'

'No. And I'm glad I didn't if it was *that* strong,' laughed James. 'Who gave it to you?'

It was waiting for me in my cabin with the welcome-aboard card.' She suddenly became very confused as she looked at her bedside cabinet. 'That's funny.'

'What is?'

'The glass and the card have gone. I don't understand it. And why didn't you get one?'

James sounded equally confused as he asked, 'Are you sure you didn't dream all this? I mean, glasses and cards don't just disappear.'

Susie thought for a moment, then reluctantly said, 'I suppose I must have done.'

'Would you rather give our drinks date a miss?'

'Did we have a drinks date? I thought you said you would phone me.' She still sounded confused.

There was a laugh in his voice as he said, 'I *am* phoning you.'

'Oh, James. You must think me a real nutcase.'

'Not at all. Just tell me one thing, will you?'

'What?'

'Are you always like this when you wake up?'

She felt there was more than just a casual question being asked. 'Why would the way I am when I wake up be of interest to you?' She wished she hadn't asked when an embarrassed silence followed.

'Just a silly question,' James said awkwardly. 'About that drink. The offer's still on.'

She was glad he asked her again. 'Give me half an hour.'

'Great. The quiet bar?'

'The quiet bar.' She hung up feeling stupid and decided to shower rather than bath, hoping it would clear her head and make her feel normal again. Tonight was a formal night and she would wear the blue dress as Carol suggested. What would James look like in a dinner suit? One thing was certain, he was sure to look very handsome. As she showered, she thought of Mark Sutherland and imagined him also in a dinner suit rather than the casual clothes she'd only ever seen him in. Susie quickly turned the shower to cool for just a moment, hoping that her thoughts of the two men would go away.

Erik de Jager's associate on board the *Verna Castle* was not happy at the way his idea had failed. He'd allowed enough time for the drugged drink to take effect, but when he entered Susie's cabin she was obviously not completely unconscious as he had planned. She had moved and made a grunting sound as he crept in and he was frightened she might suddenly wake and see him. He decided to play it safe and search her luggage while she was at the cocktail party. He knew he was becoming too anxious to get his hands on the package, and should have been patient enough to give her the drink later, as he had originally intended. Now he must not do anything to ruin his plan. He had carefully picked up the glass with the welcome-aboard card, and left, closing the door quietly behind him.

Susie walked into the bar hoping that James would be there to admire her new dress, but he wasn't. At that moment he walked in, just like the picture she had conjured up in the shower. He looked just like George Clooney in his lovely midnight-blue tailor-made suit, and she was so busy admiring him that she forgot her own appearance, until he spoke.

'Wow. You look gorgeous. Sorry I'm late. I hope you've not been waiting long? I got a call from the UK just as I was about to leave the cabin.'

'I've only just walked in. Your call wasn't bad news I hope?'

'No. Someone couldn't find a document and I seem to be the only person in the world who knew where it was. Are you feeling all right now?'

Susie looked embarrassed as she smiled and said, 'Fine. I don't know why I dreamed all that about the complimentary drink though. I really felt as though I'd been drugged when you telephoned.'

'You must have been more tired than you realized. Never mind. As long as you're OK now. Let's sit over here, shall we?'

They ordered their drinks and then James said again, 'You look fantastic. That's a great dress.'

She gave a broad smile. 'Why thank you, sir. And may I say you are looking extremely smart yourself.'

He gave a nod. 'Well, thank *you.*'

For a moment they just looked at each other and Susie got slightly embarrassed. 'You have very penetrating eyes, James.'

He moved his gaze. 'Sorry, I just can't take my eyes off you. Are you for real?'

She loved his flattery but at the same time felt uncomfortable, and for a moment wished she was under that cool shower again. 'Is it warm in here or is it me?'

He rested his hand on hers as he said, 'Are you feeling like I'm feeling?'

She withdrew her hand from his and said, 'I'll be fine. Here come the drinks.'

The steward put the drinks on the table and James signed for them. He picked up his glass and gave a toast. 'Here's to Lisbon and our visit to Sintra.'

She responded by raising her glass. 'To Lisbon.'

As the time before dinner progressed, she was disturbed by the powerful feelings that she had. This was a ridiculous situation, she thought. Here they were, two people who had only just met and already she was in danger of getting involved again, just as she had with Paul, and what a mistake that proved to be. As much as she wanted James to touch her, and as much as she wanted to get to know him better, there was a logic that told her to play it as cool as possible. She wasn't prepared to give herself the problem of finding out that a man she liked was not in fact, the person she'd believed him to be. She didn't want to go through that again.

'Is something wrong?' James was obviously worried by her sudden change of mood.

'No, of course not,' she lied. 'What made you ask that?'

'You seem different,' he said with a quizzical eye.

Tell him the truth, Susie, she thought. Don't be a stupid female and pretend. Tell him the truth and avoid any nasty moments later. 'To be honest, James. I think we might be ... oh, how can I put it? Well, getting carried away by everything that's going on. We may never see each other again when this cruise is over. No, that isn't what I meant to say. What I mean is, oh I don't know.'

He gave her a bewildered, little boy lost look as he asked, 'Yes?'

'Oh, please don't look at me like that. I really think we should try not to rush things.' She finally said it and felt better. 'You do agree, don't you, James? I mean, it makes sense, doesn't it?'

She hoped he was going to agree and not make things even more difficult. He gave her hand a squeeze and said, 'Dear Susie. I think you are absolutely right.' She was relieved, until he added, 'But we can be good friends, can't we?'

'Of course,' she said with a friendly smile, believing that with James it would be all or nothing. And even as she spoke, she hoped it would not be the latter.

As they drank, she wanted an excuse to leave so that she could compose herself. She didn't want this feeling to get any stronger. She needed a break before they sat together at dinner. Once she was at the table there would be Carol and the Westons to keep her mind occupied on things other than James. He put down his drink and said, 'I thought you were going to take some photographs tonight.'

He had given her the perfect excuse. 'Oh damn. I knew I'd forgotten something.' She finished her drink and stood up. 'I brought my old SLR, pre-digital, it's great for portrait work. And I need a spare film. I won't be long. I'll see you at the party or our table.'

When Susie arrived back the room was full of people. Susie took a glass of sparkling wine, and stood listening to the music. Suddenly, she had that feeling of being watched again, and decided to cross to the other side of the room. As she turned to look back, she was sure she saw the little man who always seemed to stare at her, mingling with the crowd, trying not to be seen. Her discomfort was relieved when she saw Mark Sutherland walking towards her.

'Hello.' He smiled. 'May I join you?'

'Why not?'

'Quite a gathering, isn't it?' said Mark.

'Yes it is. I suppose meeting the captain is a big thrill for some of them.'

'But not for you?' asked Mark.

'Well yes. I suppose it's nice to have a photograph with him but I would have thought the regular cruisers would get fed up having to queue to meet the captain every time they go on a ship.' Susie saw the little man staring again and tensed.

'Are you all right?'

'Sorry,' Said Susie. 'There's a strange little man who always seems to be staring at me and he makes me feel very uncomfortable, that's all.'

'Which little man?'

As Susie went to point him out, she found he'd disappeared again. 'He's gone now,' she said.

Carol appeared as if from nowhere and was obviously intrigued by Susie's male companion. 'Now where did you find this handsome man, Susie? Will you introduce me or are you keeping him to yourself?'

Susie could sense that her presence was about to be unwelcome as Carol's eyes fixed on Mark. 'Mark Sutherland. This is Carol Mason,' said Susie. 'Mark and I did a photo session together last year.'

'I envy you having a session with this hunk, Susie. I must learn to be a photographer,' said Carol provocatively.

'I'm sure the last thing you need to have a session with is a camera,' said Mark in a suggestive tone.

Susie was relieved to see James enter the room. 'Will you excuse me? I think James is looking for me.'

As she left, Mark and Carol didn't appear to notice her leave. Susie managed to join James just as the captain was about to introduce his senior officers. And while he did so, Susie could see that Mark and Carol seemed more interested in each other than anything the captain said.

During dinner the conversation flowed and everyone was having a good time. So Susie felt the time was right to say, 'I'm going to take some photographs while I'm on board and try to get them accepted for a magazine or brochure. If you've no objection, I'd like to take one or two of our table.'

Sybil was first to show enthusiasm and took a lipstick from her handbag and freshened her lips. 'I have no objection, my dear. Just as long as I look myself.' She fussed with her hair and then leaned over to brush her husband's into place with her hand. 'Try and look happy, dear. We might be in a magazine. I do hope the one that the ship's photographer took of me shaking hands with the captain comes out nicely.'

'I'm sure it will,' Lionel said kindly. 'Now let Susie take her photographs of us.'

While Susie was taking her pictures, she saw Mark enter the dining room. She watched as Carol's eyes followed him to his table.

'What a pity he isn't sitting with us,' Carol said quietly to Susie, raising her eyebrows.

Susie smiled to herself as she held her camera and snapped her companions. 'Just one more,' she said.

Everyone immediately repeated their expressions and after the camera flashed, relaxed once again.

'Have you planned anything special when we get to Lisbon, reverend?' James asked Lionel.

The reverend answered James with a boyish enthusiasm. 'Apart from the churches, there's a monastery I particularly want to visit. Actually, it's the architecture that we find so fascinating you know. And some of the finest you can see are in old religious buildings.'

'Yes, I agree,' said James, feigning interest.

'What about you?' The reverend turned to Carol. 'Anything exciting in your plans, Ms Mason?'

'I shall be visiting a friend. But whether it will prove exciting remains to be seen,' she said with a saucy grin.

Sybil turned to James and Susie. 'Are you young people doing anything special?'

'We thought we'd go to Sintra,' said James. 'There's an old monastery there you know.'

Susie wished he hadn't told them. The thought of Sybil and her dear husband tagging along made her feel uncomfortable. But she was soon relieved when Sybil said, 'I cannot see us being able to fit that in on this occasion, dear. Perhaps next time.'

Turning to James, Carol said, 'So you and Susie are going to sin together? Sorry, Freudian slip. I meant, Sin-tra together?' She grinned.

He was unable to hide his amusement as he replied, 'Yes. We thought it would be nice in Sin-tra.'

Not to be outdone Carol gave a knowing glance to James and said, 'I understand it's nice anywhere. But you can find out and let me know. And now, if you will excuse me, I think I shall go and have coffee in the lounge.'

As she walked out of the room with a swing of the hips, James and the reverend rose, then sat down again. The reverend's eyes were still following Carol's bottom when Sybil gave him a sharp nudge. 'Come along, Lionel dear. Let's go for a turn round the deck. You need some fresh air.' She got up and said to the others, 'If you'll excuse us.'

James and Susie were amused at the way the poor reverend appeared so henpecked, but they managed to keep a straight face as he nodded and followed Sybil like a little dog. Once they were out of earshot Susie said, 'Poor little man. He looks as though he should wear a lead with his dog collar.' They both laughed. And then Susie asked, trying to change the subject, 'How was your fish?'

'Wonderful. How was your beef?'

'Excellent.'

They both began to laugh again and James said, 'Well. That was a stimulating conversation, I must say.' He put his hand on hers. 'Join me for a coffee and brandy?'

Susie was tempted, but decided not to let her feelings get the better of her. 'Would you mind if I didn't? There are some things I must do.' His hand touching hers aroused a feeling she wasn't able to handle right now. Why did she feel so vulnerable when she was with James? she wondered. And what would their day in Sintra lead to?

He looked at her with a warm smile and stroked her hand. 'I understand you want to take things slowly. And of course you're right. But you're also wrong. About never seeing each other again, I mean. I have a feeling that we'll see each other when this trip's over.'

'Do you now?' She went to release her hand from his but he held it to his lips and kissed it. Her heart beat faster and she made no effort to stop him. She felt scared and didn't know what to do. She only knew that she was fighting a losing battle because she wanted so much to be kissed by this man. He took her hand from his lips and held it for a moment.

'I know what they say about the sea air, but this feeling

I have for you would be just the same if we were on the Woolwich Ferry.' His eyes smiled with genuine affection. 'And it isn't the five, correction, seven brandies talking. I'll see you to your deck and go straight to my bed. And don't worry, I shan't do anything that would spoil the cruise or our friendship. OK?'

Her voice was almost a whisper. 'OK.'

When Susie arrived at her cabin her thoughts were only of James. He had seen her to her deck and then left, as he'd said he would. Was he as sincere as he appeared? she wondered. She opened her cabin door and as she entered immediately had that feeling again of someone having been in there. This time it wasn't just a few things on her dressing table that were out of place. Someone had moved the pink case under her bed, and not put it back as she had left it. Her natural curiosity made her pull it out. When she opened it she could see that part of the lining had been torn away and this puzzled her. At least she was thankful that it wasn't the expensive leather bag Paul had lent her, the one the cabin stewardess had taken to the baggage room. She didn't know what to do and after some consideration, decided to leave it until the morning. After all, nothing had been taken and she could double lock her door. She got into bed and was about to put the light out when the telephone rang. It was James.

'Sorry to disturb you but I knew you wouldn't be asleep yet. I just want you to know that I've got your camera.'

She suddenly remembered that she'd left it in the dining room under her chair. 'Oh God, I'd forgotten all about it. But how did you come to have it?'

'It ended up under my chair so the table steward

assumed it was mine and gave it to my cabin steward to give to me. I just wanted you to know it was safe.'

'Thank you. I would have panicked when I realized it wasn't there. Sorry you've been bothered. I don't understand why I left it there. I've got some nice shots of our dining companions and the ship. I wouldn't want to lose those.'

'I don't think there's any film in it,' he told her.

'Of course there is, silly. I might be considered a dumb blonde but I don't take photographs without a film in the camera.'

'But shouldn't it indicate the number of shots taken, in the little window at the back?' he asked.

'Yes.'

'Well the indicator window is empty.'

Susie was getting concerned. 'Please don't tease me James. I'm really not in the mood for games when it comes to my camera.'

'I give you my word, Susie. As far as I can see, there is no film in this camera. Would you like me to bring it to you so that you can check it?'

'Yes. Yes I would. You've got me worried now. Please bring it to me.' She hardly had time to wonder if it was wise to invite a man she was so attracted to to her room late at night, when James knocked quietly.

He was still dressed and looking very handsome. He handed her the camera and as she checked it he could see that she was genuinely worried. She sat on the bed and opened the back and looked totally confused.

'I don't understand. Where's the film?'

He put his finger to his lips and closed the door. 'Shh, we don't want to wake your neighbours.'

'Sorry.' Then lowering her voice, she said, 'Someone has removed the film.' With suspicion she asked, 'James, have you got it?'

'I give you my word. I haven't touched your camera, other than to bring it here. It's ridiculous. Why would anyone want to take your film out?'

'I can't imagine. It doesn't make sense. It was with me all the time until I left it in the dining room.'

'And then the table steward found it and he gave it to my cabin steward, thinking it was mine.' James tried to make sense of the situation.

'Neither of them would take the film out, surely?' Susie asked.

'Of course not. Why would they do that?'

They both looked at each other with bewilderment. It was then that Susie decided to confide in James. 'There was something else that I don't understand.'

'What's that?'

She showed him her case and the torn lining. 'I think someone has done that deliberately. I'm positive it wasn't like that when I packed.'

James studied the lining for a moment. 'Why would anyone do this?

'I don't know.' She slowly shook her head. 'I can't explain it.'

'Getting back to the film for a moment, people would only remove it for one of two reasons that I can think of.' James became thoughtful. 'Either they are playing a prank or they don't want to be seen in a photograph.'

'But that's ridiculous,' Susie said sharply. 'On that film were just shots of the ship and our table. Not one of them objected to their photograph being taken.'

James sounded unsure. 'True. But what if someone, other than our little group, thought they might be in the picture and, for whatever reason, didn't want their photo taken?'

Susie was getting tired and confused. 'Oh, I give up. I'm too tired to think straight. All I know is, someone has messed up my luggage and stolen my film. I think I'll go to bed and hope that I wake up to find it was all a bad dream.'

James went to the door. 'Sorry I can't be of any help.' He opened the door quietly and said, 'Cheer up. See you tomorrow morning.' He blew her a kiss and closed the door behind him.

Susie went to the door and locked it, then closed the case and put it back under the bed. As she put her head on the pillow she was pleased that James hadn't tried to take advantage of being alone with her in the cabin. She wanted him to be the lovely man he appeared to be. Soon her thoughts went back to the film and the suitcase. She remembered the feeling earlier that someone had been into her cabin, and wondered what, if anything, was going on.

Before switching off the light Susie reached for her handbag to get her hankie. As she opened it she was shocked to see a roll of film that had automatically rewound on completion. Of course, if she'd used her digital camera, there'd be no fear of losing film, but she liked to use her old camera from time to time. It had to be the same roll of film that she'd shot that day! She felt both stupid and delighted, and knowing that James wouldn't yet be asleep, she dialled his cabin number. It rang only twice before he answered. 'Hello.'

'James. It's me.'

'Hello Me,' he said softly.

'You'll think I'm mad. All that fuss over the film I mean. James, I found it.'

'Where?'

'In my handbag. I honestly don't remember taking it out of the camera and I could have sworn I still had two more shots left. Anyway, I just wanted to say sorry.'

He gave a chuckle. 'It was worth every anxious moment, just to see you looking so lovely in your night attire.'

She was slightly embarrassed as she asked, 'Are you sure it wasn't you who took my camera just to have an excuse to visit a lady in her cabin at night?'

'It would have been worth it.' His voice sounded warm and sexy as he added, 'But now I'll have to think of another excuse, won't I?' The humour in his voice turned to sincerity. 'Thanks for letting me know.'

Her voice was soft as she spoke. 'You're welcome. Goodnight, James.'

'Goodnight,' he replied, then hung up.

CHAPTER FIVE

It was later that night that Erik de Jager telephoned the *Verna Castle* and spoke again to his contact on board. 'How are you enjoying the cruise?' asked de Jager, using the code, in case of eavesdroppers.

'Not too bad but I haven't had any luck in finding that little present you wanted.'

'Oh?' De Jager was surprised.

'Not yet. Mind you, I didn't have time to have a thorough look, but the shop I visited appeared to have nothing in it.'

'You are quite sure? The one I was thinking of was a very nice brown leather,' de Jager said pointedly.

'Ah. I must have been looking in the wrong shop. The one I saw was pink. Made of a fibre material.'

'There you are then,' said a relieved de Jager. 'You must have misunderstood my requirement. You will try again before Athens, won't you? I want my friend there to get exactly the gift I promised him.'

'No problem. We have almost a week before we arrive there. I'm sure I shall find just what you're looking for by then.'

De Jager felt happier. 'I have every faith in you. Oh, and

how is the lovely young lady? I trust that she is having a good time?'

'She is having a wonderful time. And looking forward to visiting Portugal with her new gentleman friend.'

'I'm so glad she's enjoying herself,' said de Jager with a sarcastic chuckle.

'I can assure you, she is. And don't worry, I'll start looking in the correct place for the leather goods.'

'Excellent. I look forward to hearing from you very soon. Goodbye.'

Bill Forward was sitting at his desk deep in thought as Sergeant Marsh came in, looking fed up. 'I've been through every blasted Castle in the phone book and every register of births, deaths and marriages I could find. And would you like the good news? I actually found a Verna Castle.' The Inspector looked up as the sergeant took out his note book and read: 'Verna Castle, 27 Milton Close. Died in 1952 aged seventy-eight!' He sat down and gave an exhausted sigh. 'It's like looking for a needle in a haystack, trying to find this woman.'

The inspector was equally despondent. 'I've had no luck either. I just don't understand how two people could be seen one day and completely disappear the next. No Susie Cunningham has gone through our ports either. So she must still be in the UK somewhere.'

'No luck with old man Lucas or the cleaning woman?'

The inspector shook his head. 'No. I don't doubt that Mr Lucas saw the girl and Julian Harper, but I've got my doubts about the Castle woman even existing. That poor mother of Susie Cunningham could have just imagined everything.'

The sergeant threw up his hands in despair. 'Now you tell me!'

'Sorry sunshine, but there it is. As Gilbert and Sullivan once said, "A policeman's lot is not a happy one".'

'I'll drink to that,' sighed Dick Marsh.

Inspector Forward got up and looked at his watch. '12.45. Time for a drink before lunch, I think. Come on, I'm buying the first round.'

Sergeant Marsh managed a smile. 'First? You mean we might have more than one?'

Returning his smile, Inspector Forward said, 'The way I feel it'll be at least three.'

The bar at the Unicorn was busy as usual. The sergeant sat at an alcove table he'd been able to grab, while Bill carefully manoeuvred himself through the crowd without spilling a drop of the two pints of beer he was carrying. He placed the glasses on the table and sat. 'Cheers.'

'Thanks. Cheers.' They drank a satisfying amount and licked their lips.

'Ahh, that's better,' said Bill Forward. 'You know, the way things are going with this case, I begin to wonder if we shouldn't just forget about a woman we think Susie Cunningham's mother knew about, called Verna or whatever, and concentrate on this Julian Harper.'

'Funny you should say that. I was only thinking about him this morning.'

Bill raised an eyebrow. 'What about him?

'Well, I was wondering whether the name Julian Harper that was on the back of the photograph was actually his. I mean, suppose it was the name of the photographer?'

The inspector saw what he was getting at and agreed.

65

'That is a very good bit of deduction, sergeant. You could be on to something there.'

'You think so?' Sergeant Marsh was pleased with himself.

'I certainly do, sunshine. Drink up and get looking for a photographer by the name of Julian Harper.'

'What about the three drinks, and lunch?'

'Like I said before, a policeman's lot is not a happy one!'

Sergeant Marsh reluctantly finished his drink and got up to leave. He turned to the inspector who remained seated. 'Aren't you coming?'

'I don't want to gulp my drink down like you just did. That's how you get indigestion.' He drank his beer slowly, leaving Sergeant Marsh wondering if he would ever understand his new superior.

Next morning, only Susie, James and Carol were at their table for breakfast. After a jolly chat, James said he had to write some postcards, Carol went to have a manicure, and so Susie decided to walk around the deck. She was on her third time round when she saw Mark Sutherland. He was wearing white trainers, a t-shirt and shorts. As he got nearer, Susie found herself admiring his physique and comparing his good looks with James's.

As Mark approached, he smiled and said, 'Hello there. Looks as though the weather will improve, and we're through the Bay of Biscay.'

'I hope so,' said Susie. 'It's what we came on a cruise for isn't it?'

'It certainly is. Good weather always cheers people up. Just look at that sea. What a difference with the sun shining on it. It doesn't look so grey and threatening now.

And it will be even better once we get into the Med.' Mark took a deep breath and said, 'It'll be lovely.'

'I hope you're right. Do you sail a lot?'

'Not a lot no. Why?'

'I just wondered, that's all.'

'Any chance of having that drink we said we'd have together?'

Susie only hesitated a moment. 'Now, you mean?'

'If you've got time.'

Susie smiled. 'Yes. All right.' Although she had told herself it was none of her business, she was curious to know why he wasn't flying to Greece.

'It's not really warm enough to sit on deck. There's a bar on the port side.' Mark took her arm and guided her to a small bar situated in a good position to sit and look out to sea. Susie ordered a Campari and soda and Mark got himself an alcohol-free lager. 'Good health,' said Mark as he raised his glass.

'Good health is something you seem to have plenty of,' Susie said. 'I suppose male models have to look after themselves. Is it a lot of work?'

'I work out in the gym a lot – even on the ship. Can't let it go. How are you enjoying the cruise?' he asked.

'Very much. But you get off in a few days, so I imagine you wish you were staying on for the whole cruise?'

'If I had someone like you for a companion I would certainly want to stay on,' he said in a flirtatious way.

Susie ignored his comment and instead asked, 'Why aren't you flying to Greece?

The question and the way Susie had asked it, took Mark by surprise. 'Why are you interested in the way I travel?'

'Most of the models I know go by air to overseas work. I was just curious, that's all.' She laughed.

Mark gave a soft laugh as he said, 'My reason for coming by ship is not very exciting, I'm afraid. The agency I'm working for in Athens gave me the choice of air or sea, and I chose the sea.' He gave a cheeky smile as he asked, 'Did I do the right thing?'

Susie was feeling slightly embarrassed as she said, 'Sorry if I sound like a nosy old woman. It's none of my business really.'

Mark suddenly asked, 'That good-looking man who sits at your table, are you two together?'

Susie was surprised by the question. 'What makes you ask that?'

'Well, you seem to be fond of each other and I just wondered if you were an item. So, are you? An item, I mean.'

'What makes you think we are fond of each other?'

'Oh, I don't know. The way you behave when you're together made me wonder. Only if you're not, do you think he'd mind changing tables with me, because I would much rather sit with you than the people I have to put up with at meal times?'

His serious expression made it impossible for Susie to know whether he was joking or not and she gave him a puzzled look. 'If you want to change places, why don't you ask him yourself and see what he says?'

Mark laughed. 'You know damned well what he'd say. Push off, or words to that effect, that's what he'd say.'

'Well, that's answered your question then. And now you must excuse me, Mark, I've got things to do.' She finished her drink and got to her feet. 'Thanks for the drink.'

'You're welcome. See you around.' He watched Susie leave and wondered why she was so touchy when he mentioned her relationship with James Kerr.

The phone call that David Anderson had hoped for finally came. His travel agent told him that they could only get him an inside cabin on a lower deck. It meant there would be no porthole but this didn't bother him. He didn't intend spending a lot of time in the cabin and at least he would have it to himself. Once he had accepted it, he asked to be booked on a flight to Lisbon the next morning. He telephoned Lisa and explained that he was being called away on business, and asked her if she would keep an eye on the house while he was gone. He didn't tell her exactly where he was going, just that it was a European trip.

He was grateful to Lisa for mentioning the *Verna Castle*. Without her he would never have the opportunity to meet this Susie Cunningham and, hopefully, get an exclusive story worth big money. David wondered what the woman was like. His imagination came up with several possibilities and while his mind jumped from one scenario to another, the thought of meeting the lady gave him a feeling of excitement that he had rarely experienced before.

He would have to use a name other than Anderson, and after giving the matter some serious thought, decided to use his mother's maiden name, which was also his middle name and appeared on his passport. And so, to Susie Cunningham, he would be David Newman. The idea of creating a new identity for himself gave him a certain thrill, and he was beginning to feel the way he thought actors do when they take on a new role. He would be David Newman, who ran an office cleaning business. It sounded such a mundane job that no one would be interested in discussing it, he thought. And even if they did, it would be so easy to make anything up on the subject. The more he thought about it the happier he felt. He would make a coffee, then begin sorting out the clothes to take with him on the voyage.

When James had finished writing his postcards, he went for a walk around the deck. The weather had got warmer and it was as though all the passengers were out to take advantage of the sunshine. He leaned on the ship's rail, and unbidden memories of Anne-Marie filled his mind.

They had met when they were students and had fallen madly in love. They were both nineteen and spent every spare moment together. She lived with her parents, who always made James very welcome during the holidays. Their relationship grew into a stable one over the following three years and they planned to marry at her local church in July. Just six weeks before the wedding, Anne-Marie developed a virus. Despite all the expert medical help that was available, the doctors were unable to save her. When she died in late August, James's life seemed to end as well.

Suddenly, his thoughts were interrupted by a familiar voice. 'A penny for them.' Carol leaned on the rail beside him, wearing a floral sari-type wrap, and a large sun hat.

'Sorry ... I was miles away,' he said apologetically.

'I could see that.' She gave a soulful look. 'I was hoping it was me you were thinking of. But I suppose it was Susie.'

James smiled. 'Actually, I was thinking of my misspent youth and wondering where the time has gone.'

'You must be looking forward to tomorrow, James? Just you and the lovely Susie together for the whole day. I believe there are lots of secret little places where you can hide in a monastery. There's no telling what you might get up to once you're there.'

'I don't think we shall get up to anything, Carol. But if we do ...'

Her eyes opened wide with expectancy. 'Yes?'

'You'll be the last to know.' He grinned.

She gave a confident smile and said, 'I wouldn't bet on it. Ciao, darling.'

He watched her walk away and wondered what it was about her that made him feel uncomfortable. Was it her overconfidence? James was certain that underneath, there was really a very lonely and insecure person. That was it, she wasn't being true to herself. Perhaps she would relax when they knew each other better.

As he walked back towards his cabin, he began thinking of what he would say to Susie when he met her at noon. He'd revealed at breakfast that his father was a solicitor. She was wondering why the son of a legal man had become a mortician and he'd promised to answer her question over a drink. He had intended to get close to Susie Cunningham. But was he getting too close? He wondered. He had an hour before meeting her in what they were calling 'their bar' which left just an hour to wait for that call from England. He was hoping the call would come soon, as he didn't want Susie to wonder where he was. Within minutes the telephone rang and as he lifted the receiver, he heard the voice of his associate in England.

As it turned out, James had to wait for Susie who was late. On the table was a freshly ordered Campari and soda. She sat and took the glass. 'Cheers.' She took a large mouthful and after she had swallowed it, gasped, 'God. I needed that.'

James watched her drink and raised an eyebrow. 'Is this my delicate, genteel, feminine date?'

'Sorry, James, but you have no idea what happened just a few minutes ago.'

'Yes I do,' he said with a straight face. 'You drank your Campari as if you were a bricklayer downing a pint of beer.'

'James, be serious. Wait till I tell you what happened in the baggage room.'

He could see that she was really agitated over something. 'All right. Just calm down and tell me.'

'One of the stewards went to fetch an old lady's suitcase from the storeroom for her and got banged on the head – but not before he saw that a bag, my bag, had been broken into. It was the better one my work colleague, Paul, lent me. He'll be furious! My guess is whoever did it was still in there and attacked the steward so that he – or she – could make their escape. So you see,' Susie continued, 'my imagining that someone had torn the lining of my other case, may not have been imagined at all. What do you think?'

He thought for a moment. 'I think it would be a good idea if you were to keep both your bags in your cabin. And by the way.'

'Yes?'

'Who's Paul?'

The question was unexpected and it showed. 'Paul? Oh, just someone I did some work for.' She wanted to tell him but not at this moment. 'I did a shoot with his models. He runs an agency. I thought I told you.'

'Yes, you told me about some models. I remember now.' He was trying not to embarrass her and changed tack. 'And we should have a look at your luggage, don't you think?'

'Yes, I suppose we should. At least it would put my mind at rest.' She hoped he wouldn't ask any more about Paul.

He said, 'It would put both our minds at rest.' Susie admired his logic and thoughtfulness, as he continued, 'This whole business is very odd. Either that, or it's a very strange coincidence.'

'I agree. I'll ask for the bag to be brought to my cabin after lunch, shall I?'

'Yes. We'll worry about it then. Meanwhile, I think we have time for another round. That is, if you can drink it as quickly as you did that first one.'

They laughed and she was now feeling much happier. As James signalled to the steward for another round, Susie reminded him of his promise. 'You were going to tell me why you became a mortician, remember?'

'So I was.'

'Well?' She waited for his answer.

He leaned in towards her and said quietly, 'Promise you won't tell anyone else what I'm going to tell you?'

She was more intrigued than ever. 'I promise. What is it that no one else must know?'

'Well, you're right. I'm not a mortician. I'm a doctor.' He watched her reaction and smiled. She was obviously not expecting his answer and was curious as to his reason for being so secretive about it.

'Then why tell people you're a mortician, for heaven's sake?'

'I learned a long time ago that, when on holiday, a doctor should never tell people what he does. Imagine what it's like to have the Sybils and Carols of this world wanting to discuss every illness they ever had. And whether they should take this or that medicine. It's the same with dentists or policemen. You never have a moment's peace.'

'Yes. I can see that. But why a mortician?'

'Because, like you, they don't want to pursue the subject.' James was amused at the expression on her face as she came to terms with this news. 'That's why, when I came to the cabin last night, I wasn't a bit embarrassed at seeing you in your dressing gown and nightdress.'

'Women in their night attire is all part of your job of course. You must see hundreds.'

He took her hand and gave it an affectionate squeeze. 'But none as lovely as you looked last night.'

She wanted to say something humorous to cool the situation but all she could think of was, 'You only said that because it's true.'

'You won't tell the others, will you?' James begged her. 'I couldn't bear Sybil giving me her medical history.'

A sudden impulse made her give him a gentle kiss on his cheek, and her voice was quiet and soft as she said, 'I won't tell anyone. I promise.'

He wanted to take her in his arms and kiss her, and she would have let him had the steward not arrived with the drinks. He placed them on the table and James took the bill and signed it. When the steward left, there was a look that passed between Susie and James. It was the look shared by two people who want to be together. And for one brief moment, they seemed to be unaware that there were other people in the room. He looked into her eyes and she returned his smile.

'Do you mind if I tell you a biological fact?' he asked.

'No,' she replied.

In a soft voice he said, 'I'm becoming rather fond of you, Miss Cunningham.'

She could feel her heart starting to beat faster as she asked, 'Are you?'

He pulled her to him and held her tight. 'I'm afraid so.'

Her eyes closed as she whispered, 'People are watching.'

The chimes, calling people to luncheon, rang out over the ship's speakers. James released Susie from his hold, and said with a nervous smile, 'Saved by the bell.'

Susie was aware that she'd been saved from possible embarrassment and was grateful to the chimes for sounding when they did. They drank up and left the bar, trying to appear casual. The bartender gave her a wink, which she pretended not to notice. Susie didn't want her relationship with James to become the subject of gossip around the ship. Her thoughts went back to Paul and how her feelings for him had been rewarded by him treating her as little more than a sex object. She couldn't bear the thought of James being like Paul and was convinced that this time it was a different type of man she was getting involved with.

Sergeant Marsh was more than pleased with himself when he put the phone down and dashed along to the canteen where the inspector was having lunch. 'We've found Julian Harper. Or at least we know where he lives.'

Inspector Forward put his knife and fork down and smiled. 'Good work, sunshine. How did you find him?'

'I went back over the models who were away when we made our first inquiries and rang two of them just now. They were in Denmark over the weekend, doing some magazine work—'

'Never mind all that. Tell me about Harper for Christ's sake!'

The sergeant sat in the opposite chair and was enjoying his moment of glory. 'Remember I showed the others the photo of Harper but they didn't know him? Well, when I mentioned his name this one I just phoned knew exactly who he was. He described him perfectly. And his real name is Geoffrey not Julian. That's why we couldn't trace him; he uses Julian as his professional name. Oh, and by the way, he's gay.'

The inspector showed his surprise. 'Harper?'

'Apparently. And the one I phoned this morning, a Stephen Conley, used to be Harper's boyfriend. But when Harper got tangled up with Paul Anderson he packed him in. Didn't sound too sorry about Anderson's demise either. Called him a nasty bastard.'

'So where does Harper live? Or are you keeping it all to yourself?'

'19 Hamilton Close, Wandsworth. Only he's not there at the moment. We found the back door open but no sign of the man himself. And neighbours haven't seen him or his car for some time.'

CHAPTER SIX

Carol was absent from the table at lunch having decided to eat from the buffet on deck. James and Susie both chose the Spanish omelette. Sybil arrived alone and ordered soup.

'Lionel won't be joining us, I'm afraid. His tummy is upset from last night. I think it was the prawns. I told him not to have them but he does love anything like that. Anyway, I got him some nice lentil soup from room service, so he'll be fine and dandy by this evening. And what about you? Have you two done anything interesting this morning?'

James could sense that Susie was slightly embarrassed by the question and answered Sybil without hesitation. 'I wrote some cards, ready to post when we go ashore in the morning. Mustn't go wasting the day worrying about cards must we, Sybil?'

'Of course you mustn't, dear. Not when you're with a pretty girl like Susie. I said to Lionel when we got to the cabin last night, it wouldn't surprise me if that young couple at our table don't get together, and he agreed. Ah. Here comes the soup.'

So much for not wanting any gossip regarding James and me to get around, thought Susie.

Erik de Jager had just received a coded call from the ship. The parcel had been retrieved and was now in an innocent-looking battered briefcase. This was good news and Erik made a call to Athens.

Dimitri Leonis was relaxing after a heavy lunch when the telephone rang. He answered it just the same.

'My dear friend,' de Jager fawned. 'How are things in Athens these days?'

There was no need for Dimitri to ask who it was; de Jager had a voice that was very distinctive. 'Very well, thank you. How are things at your end?'

'Jogging along you know. Us poor fellows in the property business struggle along as always.'

'I'm sure you manage, my friend. Tell me, is there any property that I might be interested in?'

'As a matter of fact, that's why I'm calling. You remember the property I mentioned when we last spoke?'

'Indeed I do. It sounded very interesting.'

'Well, I can either get the package to you in Athens next week, as originally suggested, or it can be with you, or your representative, in Lisbon tomorrow.'

'Tomorrow may be a little too soon. But I will see if it can be arranged and call you back later.'

'That will be fine. As long as I know before the end of the day. My colleague will be in Lisbon tomorrow and would be willing to comply with any arrangements that suit you.'

'I shall call you as soon as I can, I promise.'

'I look forward to hearing from you, my friend.

Goodbye for the present.' De Jager hung up and hoped that the package could be off the ship tomorrow. He wanted it delivered and safely out of his colleague's hands as soon as possible. The thought of it staying on board the ship for another week bothered him. Once converted into hard currency it would enable him to make even bigger deals – enough to keep him very comfortable in his old age.

When Susie and James had finished lunch, they went back to her cabin and arranged for her bag to be brought. James sat in the armchair and held out his hand to her. As she took it, he pulled her gently towards him and she sat on his lap without any resistance. He put his arms around her and she closed her eyes, so that nothing would distract from this moment. A moment that she now believed was inevitable.

As her head rested against his chest she felt a wonderful contentment that she'd never experienced before. For the first time in her life she was with a man who made her feel completely safe. They sat there for a few moments without either saying a word. Then she could feel his warm breath on her cheek, moving slowly towards her lips.

This was what she'd imagined it would be like, and as his mouth reached hers, she felt her heart race with an excitement she never thought possible. Their kiss became more and more passionate and she responded to him until she could feel herself becoming so excited that it made her frightened to continue. As she took her lips from his, he gave an understanding smile and helped her to her feet. Before either of them could speak, there was a knock at the door. Susie had to compose herself. It was the leather bag.

After the stewardess had gone, James held out his arms. She went to him and he held her for a moment and kissed her forehead. She gave him a gentle kiss on his cheek in return and then stepped back. The look in his eyes was what she wanted to see, and yet she knew that to give in to her feelings at that moment would be wrong.

'Weren't we supposed to be looking at the bag, doctor?'

He adopted a look of innocence. 'So that's why you invited me to your cabin. It used to be, "come and see my etchings". Now it's, "come and see my suitcase".' He smiled and went to pick up the bag.

'Be careful,' she warned him. 'It's quite heavy.'

James lifted it to feel the weight. 'It's not that heavy or the stewardess wouldn't have been able to carry it here.'

'Well, it felt heavy when I left home,' she said.

'It's all the unnecessary things you ladies pack,' he said jokingly. He put it on the bed then opened it. Then he began feeling the lining around the lid and inside the bottom of the bag. Nothing appeared unusual until he tapped the base. The hollow sound it gave made him react to it with suspicion. 'That's odd.'

'What is it?'

'Well, listen.' He tapped it again. 'Hear that?'

'Sounds hollow.'

'Yes it does ... I wonder?' He felt along the bottom again and managed to pull one of the corners free. He then prised what was obviously a false bottom and as he did so, it opened up as a lid with the thick quilted material lining acting as a hinge. 'Now it begins to make sense.' James sounded convinced. 'I believe something was hidden in there. Something that you weren't supposed to know about. Probably something illegal.'

Susie looked at the suitcase in amazement. 'You mean use me as some sort of smuggler! What do you think was in there?'

'God knows. This Paul who lent you the suitcase. What did you say he was?'

'He runs an agency for models.' She became worried and added, 'Among other things.'

'What sort of man is he? I mean, could he be involved in anything underhand, like smuggling, for instance?'

'Funny you should mention that. I once heard him talking to someone on the telephone and I remember thinking that he might be involved in something illegal.'

'How well did you know him? Don't think I'm poking my nose into your past, Susie, but if you've been carrying something that you shouldn't have, you could be in serious trouble.'

She tried not to appear too uncomfortable as she answered. 'I got to know him reasonably well when he commissioned me to take some photographs of his clients. We had the occasional lunch or dinner together, as you do in a situation like that. But I began to dislike him. Then, just recently I suspected him of being involved in things that weren't above board.'

'Sounds like a nice fellow,' he said with sarcasm.

Susie didn't want to hide the truth about her relationship with Paul, but she was afraid of how James might react and she couldn't risk it. Not now that she had found a man who made her feel so special. Even if their relationship turned out to be just a cruise romance, she didn't want it to end just now.

'Let's look at this thing logically.' James went over all that had happened. 'You found the lining of your own case had been torn. We assumed it was just accidental. But if it wasn't, it means someone got into your cabin, trying to find whatever it was that they thought was concealed in it. Then, once they realized that there was a second case they guessed it must be in the luggage room and went looking for it. The young steward innocently wanders into the luggage room and, before he knows what's happening, gets knocked unconscious. Does that make sense?'

'Yes. And if you're right, perhaps I hadn't imagined the welcome-aboard drink in my cabin that made me feel drugged. And it means that somebody has a key to my cabin, and that frightens me.'

'These magnetic card keys can easily be changed. They can give you a new combination at the reception desk, and that's exactly what you must do. Meanwhile, we must find a new home for this bag. It's too large to go under your bed and I don't think you want to keep falling over it every time you go to the bathroom.'

She liked the way James was taking charge. 'Can't it go back to the luggage room?'

He hesitated for a moment. 'I suppose so. Unless ...'

'Unless what?'

'Suppose this person was planning to return something else into that false compartment? Something they wanted you to take back into the UK?'

She began to see his point and became nervous. 'Whoever it is that is doing this has got to be someone on board who may come looking for the bag again.'

'Don't worry. I'll put your bag in the one place they won't think of looking for it.'

'Where's that?'

'My cabin.'

'But suppose they find out where it is and beat you on the head?'

He smiled at her concern. 'I'm a doctor. I'll put something on it.'

'When I get home I shall give Mr Paul Anderson a piece of my mind. How could he do this to me? The bastard.'

'Stop worrying. You go to reception and ask them to change the combination. Just in case someone has a copy of your key. I'll take the bag and meet you on the sun deck. OK?'

'OK.' She liked the way he made her feel safer. As soon as he had left she made her way to the reception desk. It was then that the thought occurred to her: wouldn't the most likely person to have a key be a member of the crew? And then she realized that no matter what combination they changed her card to, anyone with a pass key could still get in to her cabin. Susie began looking at everyone in uniform with suspicion, as she wondered who it was on board that had let themselves into her cabin and what exactly it was they were looking for.

Chief Inspector Murray was walking towards his office when he saw Bill Forward. 'Come into my office will you, Forward?' he called.

Forward gave a nod of acknowledgement, went into the office and closed the door.

'What news on the Anderson case. Have you got any further with it?' CI Murray asked.

'We are still hoping for a response to our all ports warning, but nothing so far, sir.'

'So your suspects could still be in the country?'

'It's possible. But why we've had no sighting of either is

a mystery to me. The girl is a gorgeous blonde: anyone seeing her isn't likely to forget her. And the man is apparently very good-looking, so if they're together, *someone* would remember them. The only person who would know where her daughter has gone is her mother. But she is suffering from dementia and isn't much help, I'm afraid.'

'Yes. I read your report. Bloody shame. Pity you haven't got a photograph of the male suspect. Any chance of getting one?'

'Sergeant Marsh is still trying, but so far, no one seems to know the man. To be honest, sir, we're not getting very far with this one.'

'Well keep digging. Something's bound to turn up. I know you, Forward. You won't give up until it comes together.'

Bill Forward gave a sigh. 'I hope you're right.' He left his superior's office feeling he had missed something in his investigation. Something his gut feeling told him he should have thought of earlier, and that annoyed him.

When Susie arrived on the sun deck, James had already prepared two chairs with towels laid out over the mattress. He waved to attract her attention and she joined him.

'Carol's on the other side of the deck so I thought over here would be quieter,' James told her.

'This is fine. I don't think I could take much of Carol at the moment. I got the key done, just as you said. You should see the way they do it. A number is punched into a machine and suddenly, out pops the new piece of plastic.' She saw him grinning. 'Oh, but you knew that already I suppose.'

'Yes. But I like listening to you enthuse over a piece of plastic. I managed to get the case into the second wardrobe by the way. I stood it on its end so that the door closes. I've covered it with the blanket from the spare bed.'

'You've got two beds and two wardrobes! And there's poor old me with only one of each. I shall have a word with the captain about this,' she joked.

James became serious as he said, 'If only we knew who the culprit is.'

Susie looked thoughtful. 'There was a strange man staring at me in the shop the other day. Then yesterday, as I was taking pictures, he appeared to hide his face with his book, as though he didn't want his photograph taken. I think it was him I saw staring at me again at the captain's cocktail party.'

'Really? You must point him out when you see him again,' said James.

'After I had the new key, I realized that anyone with a pass key could still get into a cabin if they wanted to. No matter what new combination was on it,' Susie told him.

'The truth is, it's so easy for anyone to gain entry to someone's cabin during the first full day on board a ship. All they need to do is pretend that they have left their key in the cabin or somewhere. They can ask any cabin steward to open the door for them. We're all new faces on the first day and if you bluff your way, anything's possible. Anyway, you can relax now. You've got your new key and the case is safely hidden. Sit back and forget about it,' said James.

As she lay back he did the same and reached for her hand. She lay there thinking how strange it was not to worry about him holding her hand in public. Only two

85

days ago she would have been most indignant at such an attempt on his part. Now it seemed a perfectly natural thing to do.

'You told me you were an only child, but what about your parents. What do they do?' James asked.

Susie hesitated for a moment before answering sadly, 'My real father died when I was very young. My mother remarried and, well, the man she married was horrible. I hated him and even wished him dead when I was younger. Anyway, my mother and I loved being together, just the two of us. That's when I saw her looking really happy and having fun. Then, just over a year ago, she began forgetting things. Just little things but I could see that it was worrying her. I asked Peter, that's his name, damn him, to get her to a specialist. God knows he could afford it. I had no money, only what I got from the odd photographic work, and I needed all of that to pay for the rent on a little flat I'd managed to find, not far from my mother. Anyway, the long and short of it is that an aunt died and left me a large sum of money. Well, it seemed large to me. It came to £185,000. That was when I asked her doctor if she could see a private specialist that I'd heard about, Mr Bernard Leddington-White. I expect you've heard of him?'

'I don't recall the name,' James said. 'But I can look him up.'

'He's supposed to be one of the top men in his field, and I think he must be because he's costing a fortune. He said that she was suffering from an early form of Alzheimer's and that she really needed to be in a nursing home where she would have regular treatment.'

'Where is she now?' he asked with kindly concern.

'A place in Haslemere, the Welland.' Tears came into her eyes as she spoke. James put his arm around her and gave a comforting hug. Susie sniffed back the tears and wiped her eyes on the arm of his shirt sleeve. 'Sorry,' she said as she composed herself. 'The annoying thing is, I bought my lovely flat by Wimbledon common with the idea of having my mother to stay when she got better. But somehow I don't think she ever will.' Her eyes began to fill with tears again.

He took a handkerchief from his pocket and wiped her eyes as he kissed her cheek and cuddled her to him. 'Tell me. Did her own doctor approve of the Welland and Mr Leddington-White?'

'No. He said she could see someone on the National Health but I knew there were long waiting lists and I didn't want her waiting for weeks or months, not now that I could pay. So when I heard about Leddington-White I went to see him. He said that he only worked privately and because my mother was so worried about forgetting things, I agreed that she should be put in his care.'

James was trying not to alarm her. 'And her GP was happy about it, was he?'

She became anxious as she said, 'I think he was a bit miffed that I had taken things into my own hands. Is something wrong? I have done the right thing, haven't I?'

He gave a convincing, broad smile. 'Of course you have. Now don't you worry.'

She closed her eyes and enjoyed his protective arms around her. After a few minutes, the feeling of tranquillity was broken by the voice of Carol, who had left her chair and come over to join them. 'What a beautiful picture.' She smiled. 'Mind if I join you?' She pulled up a chair and sat

87

next to James. As Susie went to sit up Carol held up her hand. 'Please don't move, darling. Unless of course you want me to change places with you?'

James found it difficult to remain polite. 'I'm afraid that having you in my arms wouldn't have the same effect, Carol.'

'You never know what effect it might have until you try it, darling. But seriously, I'm so happy that you two lovely people are hitting it off.'

James was unable to resist answering back. 'Why do I always get the feeling that you're not sincere, Carol? Could it be because you never are?'

Susie quickly tried to calm the atmosphere. 'Stop it, you two. Remember your promise to be nice to him, Carol. Please, both try and be pleasant.'

Carol smiled as she turned to James. 'She's right. I was very naughty and I apologize. Forgive me, James. Let's all be friends.'

Susie gave James an appealing glance, to which he gave a reluctant smile as he said, 'Why not.'

'Looking forward to Lisbon I imagine. You're meeting a friend there, aren't you?' Susie enquired of Carol.

'I'm hoping to, yes. Unless he's changed his plans since I telephoned him. Unfortunately, he's got a boring wife who actually understands him. Never mind. I'm sure he'll get away if he can.'

Susie was shocked. 'A bit dangerous, isn't it? Him being married, I mean.'

'I know. But he's the most wonderful lover, so it's worth the risk, darling.'

'But what about his poor wife?' James asked.

Carol grinned. 'What the eye doesn't see, as the old

saying goes. In any case, their sex life is practically extinct. I understand that she went off it years ago, the poor thing.'

Susie was confused as she asked, 'How old is she?'

'Late thirties,' sighed Carol. 'In Portugal that's old I believe. While I'm with Ramon, you two will be touring a monastery and having a wonderful time.' She winked and said, 'And if you don't then it's your own fault. And now you must forgive me, I want to soak my body in a lovely bath full of gorgeous bubbles. Ciao, darlings.'

As she walked away with everyone looking at her, James shook his head. 'I simply cannot believe that woman. I don't know anyone else like her. She's the most infuriating, outrageous person I've ever known. Imagine having her for a patient!'

Susie took his hand. 'Don't let her get to you. She really isn't as bad as she pretends. I bet the man she's meeting in Lisbon is young and single, and all that talk about a wife is in her imagination. It wouldn't surprise me if the person she's meeting is actually a girlfriend. Anyway, let's stop worrying about Carol. Isn't it time we had a drink?'

He smiled and nodded, then signalled to a steward who came to take their order.

Dimitri Leonis made the call to Erik de Jager as he had promised, but he didn't have the news that de Jager was hoping for. He'd done his best to alter the exchange of goods from Piraeus to Lisbon, but he couldn't work miracles and hoped this would be understood by the Dutchman, and not cause a problem. De Jager tried not to show his irritation at this news and remained as calm and friendly as possible. 'That is a shame, but I am sure you

did everything you could. Do you have any other sugges-
tion, my friend? Another place en route perhaps?'

'The best place is the one originally agreed. I'm aware of
every problem that could possibly arise there, and have
them all in my power to overcome.'

'I understand that. But is there nowhere else that can be
considered?' He was beginning to sound annoyed and
knew that he couldn't afford to be. 'No place at all, my
dear friend?'

'I cannot understand the reason for this urgency to
make a change of venue.' Dimitri was beginning to lose
patience. 'Has something happened that I should know
about?'

De Jager had no intention of letting Dimitri know that
one of his courier contacts had been murdered. If he
discovered that, he might not go through with the arrange-
ment. 'There is nothing, I assure you. It's just that I felt it a
shame to waste unnecessary time, that is all. We shall leave
things as planned, my friend.'

Dimitri hesitated for a moment. 'Bringing your
purchase to another venue would worry me, in case it got
damaged. I am sure you understand that I only have its
safety in mind, so please do not think I am being difficult.
Safety is, after all, of the utmost importance, don't you
agree?'

'You are absolutely right, my friend. Let us not even
worry about the matter any further. I am sorry I even
considered changing our original plan and to have put
you to any inconvenience.'

'No problem. Goodbye.' Dimitri hung up.

Erik de Jager was used to getting his own way, and he
didn't like losing. But this time he would have to go along

with it on Dimitri's terms. After all, he would soon have the product and make himself a small fortune. Even so, he was worried about the possibility of police intervention. What if they traced Susie Cunningham to the ship before it arrived in Piraeus? Or if she discovered that she was carrying his goods in her suitcase? With so many risks it wouldn't be possible for Erik de Jager to rest until his purchase was safely back in London. Agitatedly, he poured a large whisky. Was the man he had entrusted with retrieving his valuable property as reliable as he hoped? He had chosen a man who was the last person anyone would suspect of illegal dealings, and had agreed to pay him a lot of money. Money the man desperately needed to fulfil his medical ambitions. Perhaps his concern was quite unnecessary, but Erik de Jager had a nagging feeling at the back of his mind that his associate on board might not be as trustworthy as he had hoped, and with so much at stake, de Jager was a very worried man.

CHAPTER SEVEN

It was almost half past eight in the morning by the time the ship had tied up in Lisbon. The sky was as blue as it could possibly be at that time, and the temperature was already in the low seventies, suggesting a beautiful day ahead.

Lionel and Sybil had taken an early breakfast so as to be at the gangway and ready to get off as soon as permission to do so was announced. Lionel was looking at all the brochures on churches, while Sybil was searching her handbag for the passes. 'Where are they, Lionel. Did I give them to you?'

'Hmmm?' He was still studying the brochure.

'Do pay attention, dear. We need them to get on and off the ship.'

He looked up. 'Need what, dear?'

'The passes Lionel. Have you got them?'

'I thought you had them. You always take charge of those.'

'Then where are they?' She searched frantically in her bag and then stopped suddenly. 'I remember now. I put them in my pocket so that I wouldn't lose them.' She removed them from her linen jacket. 'There! You see? Quite safe.'

Lionel smiled and carried on studying his brochures.

'It's a good job I didn't let you look after them or we should never have found them. Come on, dear. The man's going to let us off.'

She was wearing a pleated skirt and cotton blouse, looking very dowdy. Lionel was in his usual clerical attire, looking the epitome of a theatrical vicar. Clearance had been given and as the gangway opened, Sybil made her way ahead of her husband, flourishing the passes at the crew member in charge of disembarkation. She hurried to a waiting coach.

'Come along Lionel. We must get a good seat so as not to miss anything.' Lionel followed obediently and climbed aboard the coach. Finding a nice seat, Sybil asked the couple behind, 'Does this go right into the centre of Lisbon do you know?'

The man answered her. 'This doesn't go into Lisbon. This is the tour to Almeirim. You want the shuttle.'

Panicking, Sybil snapped at Lionel, 'Now see what you've done. We're on the wrong coach!' She hurried off with Lionel trying to follow, but having to stop and retrieve brochures he kept dropping as he ran after her.

David Anderson had arrived aboard the *Verna Castle* by midday. His cabin was not as bad as he'd imagined. He got unpacked and settled in, then he went to the nearest bar and ordered a whisky, before looking around the almost empty deck. There were a few older people who hadn't wanted to go to the city, or were booked on an afternoon tour, and some younger ones taking advantage of the swimming pool. After a few minutes he took his drink and sat at a quiet table under a sun shade, where he could think.

Various ways of getting to meet Susie Cunningham had been thought of and then rejected. He didn't want to use the corny chat-up line, 'Haven't I seen you somewhere before?' That was definitely out. He didn't want their first meeting to be one that would make her suspicious in any way. He would have to gain her trust in order to get her talking. This meeting could prove to be extremely lucrative to him, and he had no intention of messing it up. He was determined to enjoy his trip to the full at the same time. He sat there finishing his drink, wondering what police suspect Susie Cunningham was really like.

Bill Forward had just returned from his second visit to Ruth Lewis at the Welland Nursing Home, but she had not been able to give him any new information. She was unable to remember anything regarding her daughter's whereabouts and even the mention of 'Verna' or 'Castle' got no reaction. All she talked about was her husband, the garden, and Susie coming to see her soon. She was very confused and appeared to have forgotten everything she'd told him about her daughter being on holiday.

After his previous visit, he had telephoned the stepfather, Peter Lewis, but all he got from him was a very sharp answer to his questions: 'I have no idea where Susie is and don't want to know,' was all he would say, before hanging up.

It was almost noon when Sergeant Marsh returned.

'Any luck?'

The sergeant began his account of the morning. 'My first call was on Mr Lucas. Mrs Cleave was out cleaning somewhere, so I left her till last. The old man said that he'd thought about things and felt it might be important to tell us about the girl speeding off in her car last Saturday.'

Bill Forward raised an eyebrow as he said, 'Speeding? How do you mean?'

'It seems that after she entered the flats the old chap went for his evening stroll. A short while later she came driving past him at a fair old speed. As if she was rushing away from someone. He didn't mention it before as he was afraid he might get the young lady into trouble.'

'Well, why didn't the old fool tell me this when I saw him? Did he say anything else?'

'I asked him to think about anyone else he might have seen that night but Harper and the girl were the only people he could recall seeing,' said Marsh.

'What about Mrs Cleave?'

'No joy there either. She's told us everything she knew and couldn't come up with anything that would help. She seemed very upset still. Finding him like that must have been one hell of a shock.'

'I've left a message on David Anderson's answer machine to call me as soon as he gets home.' said the inspector. 'Just in case he thinks of something he hasn't told us.'

'What about Harper's ex-boyfriend, Stephen Conley? Is there any chance that he could have been with Harper last Saturday or might know where he is? I've tried his number again but no joy.'

'He couldn't have been with him on Saturday because he was on a modelling job in Europe,' said Marsh.

'You're sure about that?'

'Yes, I checked with his agent and he confirmed that Stephen didn't get back to England until Sunday evening.'

Bill Forward shook his head and sighed. 'We've got three people we need to interview and all of them have disappeared into thin air. I tell you something, I don't believe it's a coincidence. I've got a feeling there's a lot more to Paul Anderson's murder than we imagine. And my gut tells me that Geoffrey Harper is involved right up to his neck. Even more than the Cunningham girl. But where the hell is he?'

After a morning of sightseeing and window shopping in Lisbon, James and Susie went to the railway station, hoping to get a train to Sintra that would arrive around lunchtime. James purchased their tickets and returned to Susie looking pleased with himself. 'The trains to Sintra run every fifteen minutes and it's only a thirty-five minute journey, so we shall be there in plenty of time to have lunch and relax before going to visit Palácio Nacional da Pena.'

His attempted pronunciation amused her. 'Have you ever thought of becoming a tour guide? You could make good money during the holidays.'

'I never thought of that,' he said. 'All I'd have to do is hold a coloured umbrella in the air and shout: "B tour, follow me." Hang on though. Cancel that idea.'

'Why? Don't you want to make money?' Susie asked with a grin.

'Not with a coach load of Sybils, I don't.'

She laughed, 'You're right. You stick to being a wealthy doctor instead.'

She held his arm as they walked up the long stairway that led to the platform where she saw a post box, and remembered the postcard she'd written to her mother, and posted it. She'd written a very simple message and hoped that her mother had one of her good days when it arrived.

Susie enjoyed every minute of the morning in Lisbon. And she was loving her day with the man whose arm she was now holding, even more.

The train was already at the platform and they were able to find a seat together. As the train left the suburbs of Lisbon, the scenery gradually changed, and as they neared Sintra the view became spectacular and James pointed to a huge building that stood high on a hill. It reminded Susie of a fairy castle.

'That's where we're going after lunch,' James told her.

'How on earth do we get up there? I've never seen anything built that high up!' she exclaimed.

'There's a bus that takes us to the main gate, then we get on their own transport to the palace itself. Or would you rather walk?'

'Walk? You've got to be joking.' Susie hoped he was.

'I mean from the gate to the building itself. We can get their little bus up and walk down.' He smiled at her.

'Well, thank you.'

Sintra was everything James had said it was. The pretty shops, the many varied cafés and restaurants, all created a lively atmosphere. The Palácio da Pena with its two large cone-shaped chimneys dominated the centre of the town. Dating back to the fifteenth century, it was now mainly used for classical concerts and pageants. Susie gazed at this and the nearby church of Sao Martinho and wondered if anyone else from the ship would be visiting it on their tours.

'What do you think of it?' James asked.

'It really is one of the most beautiful places I've seen. Thank you for bringing me.'

'Wait till you see the view from up there.' He pointed to palace. 'You won't want to come down again.'

'We should have come here this morning. I could spend the whole day in this place.' Susie gave a sigh of contentment.

James laughed. 'Isn't that just like a woman. If you hadn't been to Lisbon and seen the shops, you would have sulked for the rest of the day.'

She took his hand as she asked, 'Don't you want me to be just like a woman?'

'I'll have to think about that.'

Susie enjoyed the way he teased her and the relaxed way she felt in his company.

'I told you that I was thirty-two. But you didn't tell me how old you are. Or am I supposed to guess?' asked James.

'As long as you don't make me too old. Shall I give you a clue?'

'Go on then.'

'I'm between twenty-three and twenty-five.' She managed to keep a straight face as James counted on his fingers.

'Arithmetic was never my subject, but could the answer be twenty-four?'

'Yes. And it's a good job you don't have more fingers or I might have been fifty-four.' She gave a smile and asked, 'I'm not too old for you, am I doctor? Would you have preferred a young toy girl perhaps?'

Giving her hand a squeeze he smiled. 'I would say that you were just about perfect for a doctor. Having you around will keep my pulse on a good steady beat.'

Much as she wanted to hear the things he was saying, Susie didn't want her feelings to get out of hand and changed the subject. She looked at her watch. 'Didn't you mention having lunch before going to the old monastery?'

James checked his own watch. 'I certainly did. There are some nice places nearby. Come on, this way.' He took her by the hand as they walked to a quiet side street off the square.

Mark Sutherland had gone ashore to explore Lisbon and was wishing he'd been able to share the cruise with someone. But that was not a practical option because he had work to do on arrival in Athens, work that would make him a lot of money. His benefactor had insisted Mark travel alone and he had no intention of going against the wishes of the man who was paying him more money than he'd ever earned. But he knew that once he had completed his agreement, he could go on to make himself a small fortune and that was his intention. In the meantime he had to be careful and not jeopardize his plan. As long as no one was aware of what he had in mind, he was safe. He made his way back to the ship, wondering what the lovely Susie Cunningham would say if she knew the real reason he was sailing on the *Verna Castle* to Athens, and the thought began to amuse him.

James had taken Susie to a small restaurant he'd been to on his previous visit. From the outside it was just an ordinary-looking house. Inside it had all the atmosphere of a welcoming family home with an aroma coming from the kitchen that gave its visitors an appetite for home cooking.

The owner was Lino, a small man in his fifties who greeted James with a big smile.

'So you came back, just as you promised, señor. And this time you brought a lovely young lady with you.'

'We came to see if your wife is still the finest cook in Sintra,' James told him. Then to Susie, he said, 'His wife does all the hard work in the kitchen. While he serves the food, pours the wine, and charms the ladies.'

Lino shrugged. 'Unfortunately he is right. My Augusta does all the cooking and I simply pay all the bills. Now, come to this table before someone else takes it. It has the view of my garden. A view that will help you to enjoy the wine that I am about to give you. I hope you like red?'

'Yes. Yes I do.' Susie was enjoying the personal attention she was getting.

'I will tell Augusta that you are here and return with the finest Portugese wine you have ever tasted.'

As Lino went, Susie asked, 'When were you here last?'

'Almost two years ago. It was a medical convention that I got roped into. It was a chance to see Lisbon and Sintra, so I took it. Most of the others went out clubbing every night in Lisbon but it wasn't my scene. I found another doctor who wanted a more peaceful venue and we decided to have a quiet evening together. The hotel porter suggested this place and we came here three nights running. I fell in love with the town and the food here. And so, I promised myself that one day I would return. Augusta really is a wonderful cook. And Lino made us so welcome on those visits, I simply had to come back.'

'I can't tell you how happy I am that you brought me.'

Lino returned with a bottle of red wine and was

followed by Augusta. She was an attractive lady in her fifties with a big smile on her face at seeing James again.

'You remember my Augusta?' Lino asked as he began uncorking the bottle.

James stood and greeted her. 'Yes of course. How can I forget the lady who gave me those extra pounds in weight to take home with me.'

'Oh, so you came back for some more extra pounds?' She looked at Susie. 'Let me warn you, señorita, this man of yours lives only for his food.'

'Correction. I only live for your food.' Then James quickly added, 'And Lino's wine of course.'

Lino pulled the cork and turned to Susie. 'You hear that? He makes love to my wife in front of me! Just for that he can wait for his wine.'

He poured a taster of the wine into her glass and waited for her reaction. Her face was a picture of ecstasy as she sipped. 'Oh, Señor Lino. This is beautiful wine. Absolutely beautiful.'

Lino gave a smile of satisfaction. 'For you lovely lady the wine is on the house.' He winked at her. 'Even though my friend the doctor made love to my wife in front of me.'

'Come Lino. Let them enjoy the wine and study the menu for a while. I only hope they choose something I can cook.' Augusta laughed as she went back to the kitchen. Lino smiled and followed her.

Susie watched them leave. 'What a lovely couple they are. And they were obviously thrilled to see you again.'

'They made us so welcome when we came. I even wished I had stayed longer on that occasion. It's the kind of place where I'd like to spend a full week.'

'Your friend, the doctor you came here with. Where is he now?' Susie was curious. 'Do you ever get in touch?'

'No. He's from Scotland. We said that we'd try and meet up but you know how it is. Once you get home, you just never get down to actually making the effort.'

Raising an eyebrow, Susie asked, 'And does the same apply to the person you came with this time.'

James kissed her cheek. 'I didn't feel this way about Donald Mackie.' Taking his wine glass, he held it up to her. 'Here's to the beautiful girl who paid me the compliment of spending today with me.' Susie was happier now than she had ever been. And despite knowing that these ship-board romances often ended in tears, she felt extremely fulfilled. But she was unaware of the trauma that lay ahead.

David Anderson checked the passenger list for Susie's cabin number. Using his charm with the girl at the reception desk, he had made the excuse of wanting to send an invitation card for a drinks party but not wanting to invite the wrong passenger. If there was any similarity between him and his brother Paul, it was that they were both plausible liars. Something that had come easily to them since they were children.

He left the reception desk and went back to the sundeck bar. He liked the open air and was determined not to spend more time in his cabin than he had to. Without a porthole it was too claustrophobic and he only intended to use it for sleeping and changing in. After he had used his charm with the girl at reception, he hoped that she might be able to arrange a change of cabin for him.

He ordered another whisky and sat quietly thinking of his brother and how he had grown to dislike him so much.

His first memory of Paul's cruel nature was when David had been given a rabbit as a pet. His big brother was jealous of the attention David was receiving and had always found a way of hurting him. It was usually by breaking his toys or pushing him over when learning to ride his first two-wheeled bicycle. David could still remember the pain when his knees had hit the gravel path. But the worst moment in his young life was when his rabbit had been killed by an air gun. Paul had insisted it was an accident, but David knew better. He had so many memories of unhappiness because of his big brother. But now he had found a way to pay him back because, like the rabbit, Paul was dead. Just as their parents were dead, because of Paul.

His brother's murder would hopefully be the source of an income that until now, David Anderson could only dream of. He raised his glass to the sky and said with a grateful smile, 'Cheers Paul.' He was sure that this exclusive interview with a pretty killer would give him security, for a while at least. After that, he convinced himself he would make more money, one way or another.

Lisa had called in to the house at Sevenoaks to see if the place was in order, as she always did when David was away. It was the red light flashing on the telephone that caught her eye and, thinking David might have left a message on it for her, she pushed the playback button. There were only two messages. One was from the Kentish *Mercury* asking if David could cover a local carnival for their next issue, and one from Detective Inspector Forward, asking him to call Chelsea CID as soon as possible. Lisa wondered if she should telephone the inspector and explain that David was away. After a few moments' consideration she decided that it might save David a lot of trouble if she did explain that he would be unable to contact the inspector for a few days. Lighting her ninth cigarette of the morning, she dialled the number Bill Forward had given in his message. As it rang she became nervous and took an extra long draw on her Marlboro.

'Chelsea police. Can I help you?'

'Oh. Er, could I speak to Detective Inspector Forward please?'

'The inspector is out at the moment. Will someone else be able to help?'

Lisa became agitated. 'No. It's all right. I'll call back.'

'Can I tell him who called please?'

Lisa hung up quickly and went to the kitchen to make a cup of coffee. She was jittery and wished she hadn't bothered to phone. She felt uncomfortable talking to the police.

Inspector Forward was looking at a copy of Susie Cunningham's photograph. 'Where the hell are you, Miss Cunningham?' he asked the photograph.

Dick Marsh walked into the office and over to his desk. 'Did you say something, sir?'

'I was just asking this lady where the hell she is.'

'Well, wherever she is, I wouldn't mind being with her.'

'Even though she might thump you over the head with an ornamental golf club?'

'Oh, come on, sir. Look at that gorgeous face. Are you telling me that she's a killer?'

'I admit that she's a beautiful lady. But there are a lot of good-looking women in Holloway, sunshine. So never let a pretty face deceive you or cloud your judgement.

Women have been making fools of men for centuries. And I'm certain they will go on doing so till the end of time.'

'But she—'

'... Is our number one suspect at this time. Let's not forget that. Once we find her we'll soon know whether she's a killer or not.' Bill Forward put the photograph on his desk and picked up a message pad. 'What's this?'

'Oh. There was a call for you while you were out. A girl wanting to speak only to you. But when she was told you weren't here she just hung up.'

'Who took the call?'

'PC Walker.'

'But the girl didn't say who she was?'

'No. She just asked for you. According to PC Walker she sounded youngish and a bit nervous.'

'Let's hope it's the girl at David Anderson's place. Leave another message. But this time say that it's for Mr Anderson or the young lady who telephoned asking for me. You never know, she might hear it and get back to us.'

Lewis Madison was the senior partner of Madison, Coope and Lake-Smith, a firm of solicitors in Chelsea. He was going through some legal papers as executor of Paul Anderson's will, not only to organize his cremation but also to write to his younger brother David, and inform him of Paul's bequest. Once probate had been finalized, David Anderson would receive money and investments to the value of £810.000, plus a cottage in Sherborne, Wiltshire. The Chelsea apartment, plus £10,000 and Paul's Mercedes car had been willed to a close friend, one Geoffrey Harper of 19, Hamilton Close, Fulham, London.

It was later that day when Lewis Madison sat in his

armchair to relax and read the evening paper. A report on page two made him suddenly sit up. He read it carefully to make sure that he was not seeing things. After reading it for a second time he went straight to the phone and arranged to go to Wandsworth police station. There he was interviewed by Inspector Dawson, a man in his fifties.

'You said you were representing Geoffrey Harper,' Inspector Dawson began.

'I am executor of Paul Anderson's will and as such, I'm responsible for making certain that the people named as beneficiaries are the genuine and legal recipients of the deceased's estate.'

'I understand that, sir. On the phone you said that it was Geoffrey Harper you were anxious about.'

'Well yes. Yes I am.'

'In what way are you anxious?'

'I saw in the evening paper that he was found dead in Queensmere lake on Wimbledon common.'

'Yes, sir. That is so.'

'Well, inspector, Mr Harper was one of the two people named in Paul Anderson's will as a beneficiary.'

Mike Dawson became intrigued. 'I see.'

'According to the piece I read, Mr Harper had been found lying face down in the lake, and only the papers in his wallet to confirm that he was Mr Harper.'

'In other words, you want confirmation that the body found was definitely that of Geoffrey Harper.' Mike Dawson was now beginning to realize the purpose of the visit.

Lewis Madison smiled. 'In a nutshell, yes.'

'Well, apart from the papers there was a ring that has

been identified as one that he always wore. Eighteen carat with a cluster of diamonds in the shape of a heart.'

'May I ask who identified the body? You see, it is vital I have proof of his death.'

'Of course. Mr Harper lived alone and we were unable to trace any relatives. But his next-door neighbour kindly took on the unpleasant task of identification. Mr Harper's face had received a heavy blow and water can cause a distortion to a person's face. Then there was the amount of water he had taken in, plus the drugs he'd been taking. It didn't make a very pretty sight for the lady to see. Anyway, she confirmed that the clothing and the ring were his and although his face was distorted she was positive it was Mr Harper. Would you be able to identify him, sir?'

'No no. I never actually met the man.'

At that moment the telephone rang and Mike Dawson answered it. 'Inspector Dawson.'

'This is Detective Inspector Forward from Chelsea CID.'

'Hello. What can I do for you?'

'I understand that the body of a Geoffrey Harper turned up on your patch.' Bill Forward sounded concerned. 'Is that so?'

'Yes. A woman walking her dog on Wimbledon common found him in a lake early on Monday morning. Did you know Harper?'

'No. But we had a murder on our patch last Saturday night and he was one of the people we were anxious to talk to. Look, would it be possible to come over and see you today?'

'I shall be here till around 5.30. Can you make it by then?'

'I'll be over straightaway. Thanks.'

'See you later then.' Mike Dawson hung up and turned to Madison. 'Sorry about that, sir. That was an inspector from Chelsea. He wanted to talk to Mr Harper regarding a murder that he's investigating. So you're not the only one interested in him it seems.'

Lewis Madison became curious. 'I gather from your telephone conversation that this inspector is on his way over?'

'That's correct.'

'Perhaps I should have a word with him. Anything connected with Mr Harper concerns me, as I am sure you can appreciate, inspector.'

'You're welcome to wait, sir. Might I suggest our canteen? You can have some tea there and I'll call you when Inspector Forward arrives. He shouldn't be long.'

'Thank you.'

It was just after five o'clock when Bill Forward was shown into Mike Dawson's office. After greetings were over they got down to business. Bill Forward explained the rough outline of the Anderson case and his reason for wanting to talk to Harper.

Mike Dawson was sympathetic. 'I can understand how you felt when you heard that he was dead.'

'Can you give me the facts on this one? What did the post mortem come up with?' Bill Forward asked.

'He had taken at least two ecstasy tablets plus a quantity of Benzodiaphine. That's sleeping pills to you and me. Then his body had been put in the corner of the lake, and wedged under some bushes. If the dog hadn't made a fuss it could have been there another day or so before it was discovered. Oh, and there was a swollen area around the face where someone had obviously hit him.'

'What about time of death?'

'According to the report, Harper died at about midnight on Saturday.'

'Who identified the body?'

'A Mrs Elsie Markham made a positive ID. She's the next-door neighbour.'

'I know. I've met her. She was positive it was Harper even though his face was badly distorted?'

'Oh yes. She recognized his clothing and the ring that was on the third finger of his left hand. Unusual for a man to wear diamonds in the shape of a heart. Then there was his business card.'

Bill Forward asked. 'Nothing else? I mean, no credit cards or money. Nothing like that?'

'Nothing else. The killer obviously took all that sort of thing.'

'What about his fingerprints?'

'We matched them with those found at the house. Although there were only two recent sets, we matched his with those in the bathroom, bedroom and kitchen. They're the rooms you expect to find prints of the resident. The others we assume belonged to a man friend because they were definitely male.'

Inspector Forward was thoughtful. 'Was there any sign that Harper had been involved in sexual activity do you know?'

Dawson looked surprised. 'Yes. He'd had sex with someone just a few hours prior to his death.'

'Now that's interesting, because so had Paul Anderson.'

'That *is* interesting,' said Dawson. 'Oh, by the way, there's a solicitor waiting to see you. He was here when you phoned. He's also trying to trace Geoffrey Harper.'

'Is he now? I'd better have a word with this solicitor I think.'

Dawson went to the door and spoke to a WPC. 'There's a Mr Lewis Madison in the canteen. Could you show him down?'

'I do appreciate your giving me the time. I'm sorry if I'm holding you up,' Bill Forward apologized.

'No problem. Glad to be of help. You're really upset about Harper turning up like this, aren't you?'

'You could say that.' Bill Forward forced a smile. 'Harper was one of two suspects for the Anderson killing. Now I'm left with a young blonde woman. And I wouldn't mind having a word with Anderson's younger brother as well. The trouble is they both seem to have disappeared. I only hope they don't turn up the way Harper has.'

Mike Dawson felt sorry for his colleague. 'You obviously think the two killings are connected.'

'Don't you?'

'It certainly looks that way. If there's anything that I can do to help you just have to ask. The name's Mike by the way.'

'Mine's Bill. What a bloody stupid situation isn't it? Here am I trying to solve the killing of a man in Chelsea, while you've got to try and find the killer of the man who I had down as one of my main suspects.'

Mike Dawson nodded. 'You're right, it's bloody stupid. We must keep in touch all the way on this one, in case one of us comes up with something that helps the other.'

'Absolutely,' Bill Forward agreed.

The WPC came to the door and announced Lewis Madison. As Madison entered the office Bill Forward stood to greet him. 'I'm Detective Inspector Forward from Chelsea CID.' The two men shook hands, then sat down.

'Mr Lewis Madison is the solicitor interested in both the men you're interested in,' Mike Dawson explained.

Bill Forward smiled at Madison. 'Can you tell me what your work is concerning Harper and Anderson?'

'I'm Anderson's executor, and as Harper is a beneficiary, I have to be certain about Harper's death. Because in the event of Harper's death, the will states that everything goes to David, Paul Anderson's brother.'

Bill Forward showed his surprise. 'Are you saying that the share left to Mr Harper now goes to David Anderson?'

'That is correct, inspector. Although no one should know of David's legacy until he himself has been informed.'

'Would David Anderson be receiving a substantial bequest?'

'I'm afraid I am not at liberty to divulge that kind of information, as I am sure you know. Sorry, but information of that nature is strictly between the legal executor and the recipient, inspector.' He shrugged his shoulders and gave an apologetic smile.

Bill Forward returned his smile. 'Of course I understand your position. The thing is, sir, I need to ascertain who the killer in this case was. Now if Mr David Anderson had knowledge that he was to receive a substantial legacy on his brother's death, and if he happened to be in need of money, it could make him a suspect. You do see that, don't you, sir?'

Madison showed some discomfort. 'Well, yes. Yes of course. But surely he is not your number one suspect. Is he?'

'Oh no, sir, not number one. But he's certainly among them, especially if he's going to benefit from his brother's death. You see my point?'

There was a silence while Lewis Madison pondered over the situation. 'I think perhaps that, under the circumstances, I could, without jeopardizing my professional position, tell you this. Mr David Anderson will, thanks to his brother's bequest and assuming that he invests wisely, be able to live for the rest of his life without financial concern. I'm afraid I am unable to tell you more than that.'

Bill Forward had the look of a satisfied man as he smiled and shook Madison's hand.

Back at Chelsea he repeated the conversation he'd had with Lewis Madison and Mike Dawson. 'Well, sergeant. How about that? The one person we never even had in the frame is the person who stands to come out of this with big money. The younger brother.'

'It's funny, but I should have clicked that something was a bit odd the way he spoke about his brother when I phoned to tell him he'd been killed.' Sergeant Marsh thought back over the call. 'I mean, the way he told me that his brother had killed their parents. It was obvious that he hated him.'

Bill Forward sat deep in thought. 'Let's try and reason this thing out. He and brother Paul didn't get on according to David. Yet Paul leaves everything to just two people. One of them his brother, who gets the lion's share according to Mr Madison, and the other, Paul Anderson's boyfriend cum lover, one Julian, or Geoffrey Harper. Now Harper turns up dead, having been killed and dumped in a lake on Wimbledon common.'

Sergeant Marsh looked despondent. 'I had the

Cunningham girl and Harper in the frame but never dreamed that one of them would turn up dead.'

After a few minutes Bill Forward said, 'Let's look at this from an entirely fresh angle. David Anderson obviously hates his brother for killing his parents in the car crash. Then he discovers that his brother is leaving money or property or both, to a man that his brother has taken a shine to. Maybe he is disgusted to find out that Paul is bisexual. Perhaps brother David is a greedy man who decides to kill two birds with one stone. In any case, the killings have to take place on the same day and at approximately the same time. Having killed his brother, he goes and kills Harper. And now all the money will be his.'

The sergeant nodded in agreement. 'But why did he go and kill Harper on Wimbledon common? Why not kill him at his home in Fulham?'

'I must admit that's the one thing that puzzles me. Unless he *did* kill him at the house and drove the body away from there in order not to involve his local police. After all, if I hadn't known about it the boys at Wandsworth may never have tied Harper in as being a suspect for a murder in our area. I'll wait till I get a copy of the official report from Mike Dawson's department, then phone Mr Madison and tell him he can let David Anderson know that he's a wealthy man.'

'Yes. At least he won't leave the country until after he gets his legacy,' said Marsh, 'and until we've had a chance to talk to him.'

Bill Forward nodded. 'Oh yes. And I very much want to talk to Mr Anderson. Almost as much as I want to talk to our Miss Cunningham. Let's hope that her photograph gets a result soon.' His frustration was beginning to show. 'I should have been a postman.'

'Why a postman?'

'Lots of fresh air and plenty of exercise. It's a healthy life, sunshine. You never see a fat postman. Get me a biscuit and coffee, will you? I'm feeling a bit peckish.'

Sergeant Marsh smiled. 'Postmen don't eat biscuits. That's why they're not fat.'

Bill Forward picked up his notepad and pretended to throw it at Marsh as he went. Then he sat staring thoughtfully at his notes.

The view from the Pena Palace was even more spectacular than Susie had imagined. Standing as it did at the highest point on the hill known as the Serra de Sintra, it overlooked the picturesque old town and surrounding countryside.

James watched Susie behaving as if she were a child meeting Father Christmas for the first time, and her delighted expression gave him a feeling of satisfaction. 'I was right wasn't I?'

'Oh James, it's stunning. I don't think I have ever seen anything more enchanting. I feel as if I'm on top of the world looking down. How on earth did they manage to bring all the stone and everything up here to build? Did you say that the original monastery was built in 1503?' She took several shots of the view.

'Yes. Then it became a ruin until 1839, when it was restored and added to. Then it became the palace for Prince Ferdinand of Bavaria. It's all in the pamphlet.'

'I'd rather you told me.' She put her arm around him and gave a sigh. 'You said I wouldn't want to come down again. It really has been the most wonderful day. Is anyone looking?'

James turned to see several visitors enjoying the view and said, 'There's quite a few people about. Why?'

'Good.' She kissed his cheek then looked into his eyes. 'I can't remember ever being this happy. I wish we could stay here for ever.'

'So do I.' James hesitated. 'And there's somewhere else I'd like to stay for ever. And that's with you. How does that idea appeal to you?'

Susie held his hand. She knew that she couldn't hide her feelings any longer and threw caution to the wind. 'I would like very much to spend every day with you.'

James took her in his arms and they gave each other a long passionate kiss. Susie couldn't believe what had happened to her in such a short time. But she had no doubt that she had fallen hopelessly in love with this man. Nothing like this had ever happened to her before and she wanted nothing to ruin this day. But then she thought of Paul Anderson and became frightened of James's reaction if he were to learn of her sexual relationship with him.

'Is anything wrong?' asked James.

Susie excused her sudden tension by saying, 'I don't want to leave. Let's stay longer next time.'

'What makes you think there will be a next time?'

She stared out at the view and held him tight. 'Oh, please let there be a next time. There has to be a next time.'

When the taxi pulled up at the ship's gangway, Lionel got out and ran round to the opposite door and opened it. Sybil managed to hobble out with his help. Her right foot was bandaged and she leaned on the taxi while Lionel paid the fare. Her injured foot did not seem to quell her obsession for nagging her husband. If anything, it had made her worse.

'You could have done all that before I got out of the taxi, Lionel. Then I wouldn't be standing here trying to keep my balance on one foot looking like a stork. Now hurry up, dear. You'll have to help me up the gangway.'

'Just coming, dear.' Lionel was having trouble giving the correct amount of change for a tip. He finally sorted it out and gave the driver a one Euro coin.

Don Wilson, the cruise director, was about to go on board when he saw Sybil's plight and went over to the taxi. 'Can I help you, madam?'

Don was a reasonably good-looking man of around thirty and Sybil suddenly became more helpless than before. 'Oh, that is so kind of you, young man. Perhaps you could be good enough to help me get on board. My husband isn't very strong I'm afraid.'

Don Wilson was used to women like Sybil and said, 'You just lean on my shoulder or take my arm, whichever you find more comfortable, and we'll have you aboard in no time. Would you like the ship's nurse to bring you a wheelchair?'

'Oh no. Your arm will be perfectly sufficient,' she gushed.

Lionel saw her being helped and said, 'I take it you won't need me now, Sybil dear?'

'No. Don't worry, Lionel. This young gentleman has kindly offered to see me to my cabin.' Then, trying not to wince in pain she turned to Don. 'He does worry about me so. Men of the cloth are like that of course.'

Don managed to get her to the cabin having listened to

the accident that caused her misfortune in great detail. After settling her in an armchair, he offered the ship's medical service to her. 'We have an excellent doctor on board if you would like me to send him along to you. He could give you something to—'

'Goodness me, no. It's just a silly sprain. A good soak in cold water and it will be as right as ninepence. Thank you for your arm, and if there's anything I can do to help you during the cruise, do let me know. I sometimes sing for our local old folk you know,' she proudly informed him. Then to Lionel who had followed them in, 'Don't I, dear?'

'Yes, dear,' he sighed.

Don smiled politely and said, 'I'll bear that in mind. Tell me, aren't you at the same table as the lovely blonde lady and brunette one?'

'Miss Cunningham and Ms Mason, you mean? Yes, we share the same table. Why do you ask?' Sybil was curious.

'Oh, it's just that we shall be having our bathing beauty contest in a few days and I wondered if they might agree to take part. I'm sure they'd look great in a bathing costume or bikini.'

Disappointed at her own services not being required, she said with a forced smile, 'You'll have to ask them, dear. I'm sure they won't bite. Thank you again for your help.'

'My pleasure. I hope the foot gets better soon.' Don left the cabin and closed the door.

'He's right of course. They would certainly look lovely in bathing costumes,' said Lionel with a smile.

'Never mind that. Get a bowl or something and fill it with cold water so that I can put my foot in it,' she snapped.

'Yes, dear.' Lionel obediently went out, and as he did

was thinking how often his wife had put her foot in it and that made him quietly chuckle to himself.

Sybil was looking forward to the sympathy she would get at dinner, and wondered whether or not she should embellish on the facts a little, in order to make the story worth telling. Then she thought of Carol and wondered what she had done all day. It occurred to her that Carol's adventure might not be suitable for discussion over dinner. Nevertheless, she would like to know what a woman of that character actually did on her day ashore. Her thoughts went back to the mirror on the ceiling that had been mentioned earlier. Of course she could never admit to knowing why people had such things. It simply would never do for the wife of a reverend to be au fait with such things. But Sybil couldn't help wondering what added excitement it gave to see oneself enduring the sexual act, and she felt sorry that she was now too old to experiment with such experiences. Then the thought of Lionel's naked reflection on the ceiling brought her mind back to the reality of the moment. Just how long would it take him to find a bowl? she wondered.

Susan was on her way to her cabin to change for dinner. She'd been having a drink with James and another couple, a retired major and his wife, when she'd suddenly remembered something Carol had said about James at which she was still grinning now: 'Watch him, darling. He could be trying to get your knickers off.'

The lift stopped at her deck and as she stepped out she saw the man who had hidden his face from her camera and the laughter left her. Assuming that his cabin was on her deck, she wondered why he acted so strangely whenever he saw her. He disappeared around a corner but she was too shaken to follow him. Could this be the man who had removed something from Paul's bag and hit the young steward?

She sat on the bed for a moment trying to clear her head when, for no apparent reason, she thought of Lionel and the major she'd just met. One appeared to be obedient but vague about anything other than religious text and buildings. But was Lionel really as innocent as he appeared? And was Major Kenneth Dunwoody all he pretended to be? Almost certainly not, Susie decided. He was rather too keen on using old military terms that were only heard in old World War Two movies. There was something about the major that didn't ring true and Susie felt he couldn't really be trusted. It might seem a ludicrous idea, but was there anyone she could truly trust – even James?

David Anderson had given up hoping to 'bump into' Susie Cunningham near her cabin so he decided to look out for her at dinner, and went for a pre-dinner drink. As he entered the bar he noticed an attractive dark-haired woman who was sitting in an alcove, and as he studied her, was hoping that the young officer with her was not a serious date. When they got up to leave, David finished his drink and followed at a discreet distance. The officer said goodbye at the lift and walked on while the woman pressed the button for the lift. On impulse, David joined her.

'Well, if you're an officer's wife, I must join the merchant navy,' he said, hoping for a favourable reaction.

She smiled. 'Oh, please don't go joining anything just to get a wife. I'm sure you could hire a uniform if you wanted to impress a lady.'

The lift arrived and David stood back for Carol to enter, then followed her in and asked, 'Dining room?'

'If that's where you're going.' She smiled.

'Yes. And you are?' he asked.

'I'm Carol. Carol Mason.'

'And I'm David Newman. No chance we're on the same table – twelve?'

'No chance, darling. I'm sitting with my best friends, Susie and James.'

'Shame. Perhaps we'll meet later?'

'Perhaps!'

The lift came to a stop and the doors opened. He watched her walk on into the dining room. Carol was the sort of woman who challenged men, and he liked that.

Sybil's voice could be heard as she reprimanded her husband. 'No, Lionel. Don't hold me like that. Just let me lean on your arm.'

As she entered the dining room, hobbling on one leg, she enjoyed being the centre of attention, whereas Lionel was obviously embarrassed.

James got up to help, and taking her arm, led her to her chair. She appeared to be in pain and he looked concerned as she finally sat.

'Thank you, James. Sorry to be such a nuisance but it still hurts if I put any weight on it.'

'What happened?' he enquired.

Sybil told of her experience with dramatic effect. 'I was looking up at the wonderful dome of the cathedral when my foot went into a hole. I thought I had broken my ankle until a priest assured me that it was just a sprain. He was a man who had been medically trained, of course.'

By the time she had finished her story of a sweet nun who appeared to have a degree in the art of foot bandaging, Carol had to draw her attention to the steward, waiting with great patience to take their orders.

'But you don't want to hear all the gory details of my unfortunate accident,' she announced.

The others were relieved and proceeded to give the steward their orders. After he had collected the menus and left, Susie turned to Carol and asked, 'Did the cruise director approach you about entering the bathing beauty contest?'

'Yes. As soon as I got back on board he was on me like a whippet. I imagine he asked you too?'

'Yes. But I said no. I'd be too embarrassed. Besides, I don't wear bikinis,' Susie added.

James agreed. 'Quite right. I don't want lecherous old men ogling my girl.'

'*Your* girl?' Carol showed genuine surprise. What's happened? Do tell, darlings.'

Susie gave a wide grin. 'We decided to get engaged.'

'Congratulations. But does this mean that my passionate love affair with James is over?'

'Afraid so.' James smiled.

Sybil forgot her sprained ankle and despite smiling said, 'And yet you've only known each other a very short time. I hope you aren't rushing into things too quickly.' Then trying to appear pleased, she added, 'Although Lionel and I felt you were meant for each other, didn't we, dear?'

Lionel smiled. 'Congratulations to you both.'

'Pity you aren't still in business reverend,' said Carol. 'You could have had a nice little earner there and, who knows, done the first christening as well.'

Lionel was amused at the thought. 'I do think that's rather premature, Ms Mason. But if I were still "in business" as you put it, I should have been delighted to officiate.'

Susie was getting slightly uncomfortable and changed the subject before Carol went too far with her comments. 'Are you going in for the bathing beauty contest, Carol?'

'No. Like you, I declined the offer.'

'Oh, but with your figure you'd walk away with first prize for certain, dear,' exclaimed Sybil. 'No question about it.'

'Thank you, Sybil. But I'm afraid I don't show my legs. Not when I'm in public,' Carol replied.

'Why on earth not, dear?'

'When I was fourteen I was staying with an aunt in the country. I slipped climbing a stile and a rusty old nail tore into my right leg and it became infected. I had to lose part of a muscle and the scar I was left with is not one that I wish to expose to the world. Sorry, Sybil, I didn't mean to upstage your foot story.'

There was a momentary silence, which was finally broken by Carol who reverted to her old self. 'Now, do tell us everything that happened in Sin-tra.' Her voice became sultry. 'And I do mean *everything*.'

In a strange way, James was glad she had reverted to type. The atmosphere was becoming quite heavy. He was about to answer her when their first course arrived. 'Later perhaps,' he said.

'Later it is. But I shall insist on buying champagne in the bar. I'm sure you'll join us for a drop of bubbly holy water won't you, reverend?'

Lionel gave a look of regret. 'I think we shall have to say no on this occasion. Sybil must rest her foot.'

'Rubbish,' Sybil insisted. 'A drop of the happy grape will do my foot the world of good. Any doctor will tell you that champagne is the best pick-me-up you can have.' She looked at James. 'Isn't that true?'

Susie wondered how he would answer.

'Yes,' he said. 'I believe my first aid manual insists that champagne should be taken whenever a sprained ankle occurs.'

'Oh dear, I am naughty.' Carol sounded reproachful.

Thinking she was serious, Sybil asked, 'Why, what have you done, dear?'

'I've been drinking champagne all these years without ever having a sprained ankle.'

Even Lionel was amused by her remark. But Sybil wasn't too sure whether she was being made fun of or not. Susie sensed her uncertainty and tried a change of subject. 'I love your reference to the "happy grape", Sybil. I don't think I've heard champagne called that before.'

'Oh thank you, dear.' She enjoyed the compliment. 'But it isn't mine,' she confessed. It's from an old Bob Hope film.'

'We won't let on,' said Carol in confidence. 'From now on I shall tell everyone it's a Sybil Weston original.'

Sybil still wasn't sure how to take Carol's remarks but managed a weak smile. 'Thank you, dear.'

Lionel was hungry and said, 'Bon appetite everyone,' and tucked in to his smoked salmon starter. The others followed his example and began eating.

During dinner, Susie expounded the virtues of Sintra and sang the praises of Lino and his restaurant, explaining in detail the interior of the monastery, and the breathtaking views from its ramparts. Lionel listened with great interest to the description of the monastery, while Sybil was enthralled at Susie's commentary and decided it must have been a very romantic place.

Carol's concentration was interrupted when she glanced at table twelve and noticed the young man from the lift looking in her direction. She smiled in recognition, then made another effort to listen to Susie. But her eyes went back to David again and she felt strangely uncomfortable at the way he was staring. Normally she loved the attention of a young man but this time her intuition told her that there was something odd about him. She looked back at Susie just in time to hear the end of her graphic account of her day in Sintra.

Sybil wiped a tear from her eye. 'How lovely, Susie. What a lucky girl you are to be proposed to in such a wonderful and romantic place.' Then turning to Lionel, 'Remember where you proposed to me, Lionel dear?' she asked, hoping he would remember.

Lionel became thoughtful. 'Wasn't it at the church bazaar, when your mother had the marmalade stall?'

'No dear. It was in your parents' front room. Surely you can remember? Your father left us alone to take your mother to her sister's.' Then proudly to the others, 'No sooner were his parents out of the house, then Lionel took the bull by the horns and asked me. He'd been plucking up courage for ages.' She gave a nervous giggle. 'There's more to Lionel that meets the eye you know.'

'Yes, I'm sure there is,' James politely agreed.

Lionel shook his head. 'And all this time I thought it was at the church bazaar. But I'm sure you're right, dear.'

'Of course I'm right!' Then, trying to cover her annoyance, she added warmly, 'He remembers really. He just likes teasing me.' She gave him a loving pat on the knee and smiled at the others.

Carol gave Lionel's other knee a gentle pat and said, 'Why don't we all go to the bar and make Sybil's foot better?'

Lionel appeared totally confused. 'I don't quite follow.'

'Apparently there's nothing like champagne for putting it right. Ask any doctor.' She looked at the others. 'Who's for a nice glass of Doctor Bollinger? My treat.' She took hold of Lionel's arm. 'Come along, darling. James and Susie will help Sybil.'

Sybil gratefully accepted the arm that James offered and forgot about her limp. Susie took James's other arm and was feeling really happy as they walked to the door. However, she noticed a young man sitting at table twelve and, for a brief moment, thought that he reminded her of someone.

Once everyone had got their glass filled it was Carol who got to her feet. 'To James and Susie. May the future be happy and the past be but a memory. Especially the bad bits.' she raised her glass to them and gave a sincere smile. The others raised their glasses to them and drank.

James got to his feet. 'Can I just say a big thank you to all of you? You've been very kind to us. But I would like to say an even bigger thank you to Susie, for saying yes.' He leaned over and kissed her.

At that moment, David Anderson came in and sat at the bar. When Susie saw him again she suddenly realized who it was that he had reminded her of. His features and the way that he walked … it was like looking at Paul. And he was the last person she wanted to think of at this moment.

Suddenly, Carol noticed David. 'Oh, there's my lift boy over at the bar.'

'Lift boy?' Susie asked.

'Yes. He got in the lift with me and, unless I'm wrong, was trying to chat me up. Not my type though.'

Sybil studied David and said, 'Seems a nice young man. In his early twenties I would say.'

'Watch her, reverend. I think she's after a toy boy.' Carol laughed.

'Nonsense!' said Sybil. 'I wouldn't know what to do with a toy boy.'

Carol turned to Susie and quietly asked, 'When you saw my lift boy just now, you looked as though you knew him. Do you?'

'He reminds me of someone, that's all.' Susie was casual in her reply, and quickly asked James, 'Is there any more champers? My glass is very dry.'

James filled her glass and she continued chatting to the others.

Carol thought that Susie might be hiding something and was curious to know what. But for now, she decided to bide her time, and joined in the general conversation with everyone else. After a while, she announced that she was going to catch the late show in the theatre and made her apologies, then left.

There was a momentary silence, during which Susie noticed David Anderson leave the bar. Once again she thought how like Paul he was, and it made her uncomfortable. Would she ever tell James the truth about her relationship with Paul? she wondered. If he ever asked her if she had been to bed with her employer, wouldn't it be best to say no and protect the love that she and James had found together? As these thoughts went rushing through her head the sound of Lionel's voice broke her concentration. 'Before I go to bed, may I just say how happy I am to have been included in this little get together to wish James and Susie every happiness? I don't usually drink champagne but I think I could get used to it,' he chuckled. 'Here's to you both.' As he stood up to raise his glass to them, he staggered and it was James who managed to stop him falling back into his chair.

Sybil was embarrassed. 'Time we went, I think. Come along, dear.' She took him by the arm and managed to steady him. 'Say goodnight, Lionel.'

'Goodnight Lionel.' He giggled. 'And goodnight everyone. We must do this again, Sybil dear. It's such fun.'

Sybil gave them all a friendly nod and led him away with her foot having made a miraculous recovery.

'Were you serious about having an early night?' James asked quietly.

Susie smiled. 'I think I'm ready for bed. We girls need our beauty sleep. Aren't you ready for bed?'

Trying not to smile he said, 'Susie. Really!'

'You know what I meant,' she giggled. 'I really think I've had too much champagne but I must say something.'

'What?' He had that warm and loving look in his eyes and she felt the need of a cool shower again.

'Thank you for the most wonderful day.' Her heart began to quicken. 'James, please don't look at me like that or we will both end up spoiling everything and I don't want us to do that.'

He helped her to her feet and held her to him. 'I don't want to spoil it either.' His voice became a whisper. 'But I tell you this, Miss Cunningham.'

'What?'

'I don't think I shall finish this cruise without making love to you.'

She knew that if she didn't leave him now, they would end up in bed together. She wanted him to make love to her more than anything but she was afraid. What if the magic of today was to end? And how would she feel if she allowed herself to sleep with him tonight? Would he lose respect for her for being so willing to give herself to him after such a short time? Or even worse, would she herself feel cheap, the way she had after sleeping with Paul? All these thoughts were going through her mind and she was determined to keep her self-respect where James was concerned. She looked into his eyes and whispered, 'Not now, darling. I want to keep today special.' She kissed him tenderly and with her voice becoming emotional, said, 'I love you. Goodnight.'

James watched her walk away and despite his desire to run after her, remained standing there until she had gone. Just one more day at sea and then they would explore the Spanish port of Malaga together and that was when he would buy her an engagement ring. It was the thought of Susie being his fiancée, then wife, that gave him a feeling of security. He was convinced that they would have perfect happiness together.

Susie was content. The day had been so perfect and the views of Sintra from the ramparts were vivid as she lay in her bed. The photographs that she had taken would always be a reminder of this day, a day so special to her. A day that had ended with her drinking champagne with a man she had accepted as her own when he proposed to her. She wished that James was lying beside her, holding her, kissing her. She wondered why her emotions were so mixed and confused, and how people like her parents had managed to remain chaste during all those months of being engaged. Surely they must have craved each others bodies and longed to be alone together in bed. The thought of spending months without the sexual experience that she desired to have with James, was something she could not begin to imagine. Yet, she knew that when the time came, it would be wonderful. It was the comforting thought of being safely in his arms after making love, that let her drift into that dreamy state that finally becomes sleep.

CHAPTER EIGHT

Inspector Forward was in his office early. Now that Harper was dead he had a lot of rethinking to do. The Cunningham girl could not have lifted Harper into the boot of a car, if she were the killer. If the killing had been done at the house she would have needed an accomplice. His thoughts went to David Anderson. He could have lifted Harper and put him in the boot of a car. He might even be in cahoots with the girl and they could give each other a firm alibi for Saturday night. He didn't really know what to think, and was sitting in his chair letting his mind conjure up any possible connection he could, when the phone rang. It was Inspector Mike Dawson.

'Morning, Bill. I thought you'd like to know that after you came yesterday I decided to send two of my men back to the Harper house to see if they could find anything that we had missed, bearing in mind that we had no idea of your interest at the time of his death, and our search was mainly for any weapon and signs of forced entry etc.'

'Of course. And did you find anything?'

'Yes. His diary. It was in a holdall with his overnight things. He obviously kept it hidden from everyone else and having read some of it I'm not surprised. Once forensics have finished checking it out I'll send it over. I think the last few entries will interest you.'

Bill Forward was more than grateful. 'Many thanks, Mike.'

'You're welcome. We've got to keep each other up to date. I'm sure you'd do the same.'

'How soon can I see it?' Bill Forward asked anxiously.

'Some time later today. I'll give you a bell as soon as I get it.'

'I shall look forward to reading it. Cheers.'

After they hung up, Inspector Forward felt that at last things might be turning in his favour.

Geoffrey Harper's diary arrived just as Bill Forward was thinking of going home. The forensic department had given Mike their findings. There was only one set of prints found on it and they matched with those taken from the house. They were now officially those of Geoffrey Harper. He sat and flicked the pages until they showed the final entry. It read: 'Why is Paul beastly to me since he knew that Stephen and I were together? Why is it that I cannot have a simple life? Why is Paul being so difficult?' It was dated Thurs, 20. 9 p.m.

He turned back a page and read the entry for Wed, 19. 10.30 p.m. 'I've developed a terrible shake and can hardly hold the pen as I write. Why was Paul so preoccupied today? What is happening to him? I hate this secrecy and want him to be more open with me. I think that my relationship with Stephen is upsetting him. Why won't he listen to me? Why can't we all be friends?'

Turning to the page dated Tuesday, 18. 2 p.m., he read: 'Frightened to death that I might have the dreaded. Waiting for the news from the hospital. Well, if I have it and have to die from it I'll spread it around a bit first. I'm terrified of this horrible thing and need loving more than ever now. I wish I wasn't afraid of what might happen today.'

As Forward flicked through more pages and read the odd entry it struck him that everything he read was from the hand of a dangerous man. He was feeling too tired to read any more and locked the diary away in his cabinet. Tomorrow would be soon enough to go through it properly. He put on his coat, switched off the light and closed the door.

As soon as he left the office he heard the phone ring. He hesitated for a moment, considering whether to go back in and answer it. He decided against it as he was really tired and wanted to get home. He knew that whoever it was would ring again in the morning if it was important.

Lisa Martin had played the answerphone messages and when she heard a second one from the police, plucked up courage to phone them back. She let it ring for quite a while and then hung up, relieved that no one answered. She might try again tomorrow and find out what they wanted, she thought. Then poured some whisky into a glass and lit a cigarette. She switched on the television and sat comfortably in David's cottage, wondering where he was and what he was doing. By the phone she'd seen his notepad with the words 'Verna Castle' written on it. He must have written it down after she had told him about it. She folded the note paper and put it in her handbag. She tried concentrating on the television programme but her thoughts went back to the *Verna Castle*. Was David planning a cruise on it? she wondered.

And if he was, would he take her with him? The thought of being with David on a ship excited her and she began convincing herself that this was what he was planning. A surprise holiday for just the two of them. She sat back in the chair imagining herself on a big liner, and spent the rest of the evening wondering what part of the world they would be going to, and dreaming up pictures of exotic places. She looked forward to David returning from his business trip, so that he could tell her all about his plans for the surprise holiday.

Inspector Forward was reading the diary and was curious as to how anyone could write such personal things. Surely they must realize that one day someone else would be reading this record of their private thoughts. It was as he turned back the pages to the previous month that he noticed something strange about the handwriting. The up-to-date entries struck him as being different. And not just because of the shaky hand of the writer.

The office door opened and Sergeant Marsh came in. 'Good morning, sir.'

'Morning.'

'Is that the diary you're reading?'

'It certainly is. I want you to have a look at it and tell me if anything strikes you as strange.' He passed the diary over.

The sergeant read the first entry. 'Blimey! Not exactly the book at bedtime for grandma, is it?' He turned a few pages. 'I could never write a diary. I'd always be afraid of someone else reading it.' Listen to this. "My day was ruined by the news of Roger's illness. I cried myself to sleep. Why can't we make love without the fear of Aids?

Life is so unfair … God bless Roger and make him well."
A bit yucky, isn't it?'

'Have a quick look through and then turn to the last
pages and see what you think.' Bill Forward watched with
interest as Sergeant Marsh glanced through the diary.

It was after a few minutes that Marsh read the last pages
and turned back to some earlier entries. He returned to the
final pages again and looked puzzled. 'That's odd,' he said
thoughtfully.

'What strikes you as odd?' Bill Forward was interested
in the answer he would receive.

'Well. It's obvious isn't it?'

'What is?'

'All the earlier entries mention this Roger. Then
suddenly it stops mentioning him and it's all about Paul.'

'Correct. So where are we now?'

'Well. All we know for sure is that Susie Cunningham
was possibly involved with Paul Anderson's death. That's
because she was seen leaving his flat around the time that
he was killed.'

'Correction. She was seen leaving the building, not flat
six.' Bill Forward was thoughtful. 'I've got a feeling that
we are doing exactly what the killer wants us to do.'

'What's that?'

'Make bloody fools of ourselves.'

'But I always said that Susie Cunningham wasn't a
killer. At least, ever since I saw her photograph I did.'

'I know. I know. But, as I said, never assume when it
comes to pretty women, sunshine.'

'But surely you don't really think …'

'I don't know what to think. And that's the truth. Until
this diary turned up I would have believed that Geoffrey

or Julian Harper and Susie Cunningham were still the best bets as far as suspects go. But now? Christ knows what I believe.'

Sergeant Marsh tried to think logically. 'Let's look at the facts, sir. Harper and the girl were seen leaving by old man Lucas. He was positive about that, even to the time that they were seen. Suddenly, Miss Cunningham disappears and so does Julian Harper. Then, while we are looking for a Verna Castle, who, according to the mother, Susie Cunningham has gone away with, we find that Harper has been dead all along. Killed and dumped in a lake on the same night as our first victim, Paul Anderson. And now we've got this diary.'

The telephone on the inspector's desk started to ring. He picked it up and answered. 'Detective Inspector Forward.'

'Hello. There was a message on the answering machine for one of us to call you,' Lisa Martin said nervously.

'Is that the lady who phoned yesterday, when I was out?'

'I did call yesterday, yes.'

'We're talking about the message that was left on Mr David Anderson's machine, I take it?'

'Yes.' She sounded more nervous.

Bill Forward spoke in a friendly voice. 'It's good of you to call Miss, er …?'

'Martin. Lisa Martin. I'm David's girlfriend.'

'Well, it's nice of you to call Miss Martin. I wonder if you can tell me where Mr Anderson is, only I think he can help us with some inquiries that we're making.'

'He's away on business at the moment, sir, but I don't know where exactly.' She was sounding more relaxed. 'He

could be anywhere. He usually phones to tell me when
he's coming back so as I can get his house ready for him.
Tidy it up, I mean.'

'I see. Well if he phones, would you please ask him to
give me a call? You've got my number.'

'Yes. Yes of course. He's not in any trouble, is he?'

'Oh no, miss. It's just that I need some information and
he might be able to help me.'

'Oh, I see.' She sounded relieved.

'By the way, Miss Martin. If I should want to contact you
again, what's the best way to get in touch with you?
Should I ring Mr Anderson's number or is there another
one I could try?'

'I share a flat with a girlfriend.' She gave him the
number.

'Thank you for your help, Miss Martin. I appreciate you
taking the trouble to call. Goodbye.'

'Goodbye, sir.'

Bill Forward hung up. 'That was young Anderson's girlfriend. She's no idea where he is but said he usually calls
before he returns home. We shall just have to wait for her
to pass on my message to him.'

Susie had just stepped out of the shower when her telephone rang. She threw the bath towel around her and
rushed to pick it up. 'Hello?'

A throaty voice answered. 'Hello, lovely.'

'James? Is that you?'

'Yes, darling, it's me.' He coughed. 'Sorry about that.
Look, I won't be joining you for breakfast. I seem to have
picked up a virus and I don't want anyone else to catch it.
Least of all you, sweetheart.'

'Oh James, I am sorry. Can't I come and see you later?'

'No, Susie.' He coughed. 'Better leave me to suffer it on my own. And before you ask, yes, I have seen a doctor.'

'You have? When?'

'In the mirror this morning.' He went to laugh but started to cough. 'He doesn't look too good either.'

'Oh James. What is it you've got? Do you know?'

'One of those bugs that goes around. I could have picked it up yesterday somewhere. Even from the air conditioning.'

'So what are you taking? Have you got something with you?'

'My cabin steward is getting me something from the shop. I shall be a good patient, I promise. Now go and enjoy a good breakfast and don't worry.'

She was upset but tried to sound cheery. 'I'll telephone you later, shall I?'

'No. Let me call you. I'm going to sleep as much as I can and let the medicine do its job.' His voice sounded tired.

'All right, darling. Get well very soon. I shall miss you all day.' She blew a kiss. 'Love you.'

'Thanks. That's the best medicine you could give me. Now run along and give my apologies to the others.'

'I will.'

'Bye, Susie.' He hung up.

She put down the phone and suddenly that lovely feeling she'd had when she woke up, vanished.

David Anderson had abandoned his idea to explore the ship and decided to make a straightforward approach to Susie. After all, he knew from his meeting with Inspector Forward that she was a photographer. What better way to introduce himself than as someone who had seen her work somewhere. Besides, he knew her name and that would be quite a convincing point in his favour. As long as he didn't make it sound like a chat-up, he would be home and dry.

When he got to the dining room he went to the restaurant manager and said in a confidential way, 'I wonder if you can help me?'

'If I can, sir.' The restaurant manager saw the ten pound note in David's hand and was prepared to be as helpful as he could be.

'Well, it's a bit embarrassing. You see, a friend of mine has asked me to say hello to a friend of his, but the trouble is I haven't a clue what the lady looks like.' The note was passed surreptitiously from hand to hand. 'The lady's name is Susie Cunningham.'

'That's Miss Cunningham just coming in, Mr Anderson.'

When David saw the gorgeous young lady he was taken aback. 'Good lord. She's not at all the old frump I had imagined. Well, thank you very much.'

'You're more than welcome, sir. Anything I can do, you only have to ask,' he said, carefully pocketing the note.

'Just one other thing,' David said quietly. 'I am known by my business associates under my professional name, Newman. So if you could remember that, I would be grateful.'

'Of course, Mr Newman. I fully understand.'

David went to his table and having sat and exchanged the usual greetings with his companions, he noticed that Susie was the blonde sitting next to the brunette he'd encountered in the lift. Apart from the elderly vicar and his wife, he was trying to recall who else he had seen at that table. Only a good-looking man, as far as he could remember. David hoped that the man wasn't involved with either of the young women. If he was, then he would cross that bridge when he came to it. Meanwhile, he would wait for the right moment to carry out his plan to meet Susie Cunningham face to face. But having seen her, he began to think that his exclusive interview with a murderess was just a pipe dream. He couldn't believe that this lovely girl could kill anyone. But having come this far, he intended to find out, just in case. Besides, he had paid for the cruise and intended to enjoy it.

The Westons were sorry to hear of James's sudden illness and even Carol sounded genuinely concerned.

'When you speak to him, give him our best wishes.'

'Thank you, I will.' Susie sighed. 'It's funny, isn't it? I didn't even know him a few days ago. Now I feel strange when he isn't with me.'

'That's what love does to you, darling.' Carol smiled. 'When that happens to a girl all feelings of reality disappear.'

'You speak from experience I take it?' said Sybil.

'Oh yes.' Carol became dramatic. 'I've been there, Sybil. I wish I hadn't been there so many times, but I have. I know only too well how dear Susie is feeling. You too may have been there. But you probably can't remember that far back.'

Sybil refused to be goaded and just smiled at Susie. 'Tell James that we want him to rest until he's fit and well again and I think we will send him a bottle of bubbly to perk him up.'

'Yes indeed. Nothing like champagne for perking you up, as I found out last evening.' Lionel gave a cheeky grin.

'In your case, Lionel, it perked you down,' Sybil said with a stern look. 'He's not used to it, you see,' she informed Susie.

'But I could get used to it,' he chuckled. 'And by the way, Ms Mason, thank you for escorting me last night. It was a moment I shall always cherish. All the men envying my being escorted by a beautiful young woman.'

'Don't embarrass her, Lionel.' Sybil felt awkward. 'It's the drink talking of course. The effect hasn't worn off yet.'

'He didn't embarrass me, Sybil.' She gave Lionel a light slap on his hand. 'You're a naughty boy to go upsetting your lovely wife like that.'

Sybil once again decided to say nothing. Knowing that she could never beat Carol in a contest of repartee.

Susie was in no mood to join in the banter and ordered a poached egg, rather than a full breakfast.

When the others had eaten the Westons were the first to leave, saying a warm goodbye to Susie. But Sybil simply gave a polite nod to Carol as she went, while the reverend smiled at both ladies, almost in defiance of his wife.

'I think I must have upset the old bat. Can't think why. I was only trying to explain why a man would rather be seen in my company than in hers.' Carol sounded hurt.

Susie gave a knowing look as she said, 'You really love it, don't you?'

With an innocent look, Carol asked, 'Love what, Susie?'

'You know damned well what. Making people feel embarrassed and watching them squirm, that's what.'

With theatrical surprise, Carol said, 'Oh. I don't, do I?'

Susie couldn't resist laughing. 'You really are the end.'

Carol smiled. 'Well she really is a silly old bat. I'll bet she's not as innocent as she pretends.'

'Carol! What a thing to say.'

'It's true. Look at the way she is with James. Looking at him, wishing she was thirty years younger.'

Susie's mouth dropped open. 'You're not serious!'

'Of course I am. She could probably teach us a thing or two.'

'I can't imagine anyone trying to teach you anything where sex is concerned.' Susie gave an incredulous glance, then drank her coffee.

Carol had a wicked twinkle in her eye. 'I bet James is not ill at all. I think he's waiting for Sybil and they're going to have an orgy in his cabin.'

Susie chuckled. 'James and Sybil. Could you just imagine?'

Carol got up to leave. 'The mind boggles. If you get lonely without lover boy, I shall probably be on the sundeck until noon. After that, who knows? It all depends on which man has the nerve to invite me for a drink, or something. Meet you in the Neptune bar around midday. Ciao, darling.'

Susie finished her coffee and wondered how James was feeling and whether he would be fit enough for their day in Malaga the next day. As she sat there day-dreaming of James and herself, there was a sudden sound of crockery being collected and she could see that most people had left the dining room and that the stewards were clearing the tables. As she was walking out of the dining room another thought came to her. Would she send another postcard to her mother? This time a romantic view of Portugal or Spain? Anything to hopefully give her pleasure to look at.

She knew that a carer would read it to her, even if she was having one of her bad days.

Susie wanted so much to see her mother well again. She wished that she could tell her about James but knew it would have to wait until she returned. It would only confuse her mind to explain that her daughter had found a man she wanted to marry. But heartbreaking though it was, she had to accept that her mother might never be well again.

In her cabin, she chose one of the complimentary post-cards in the stationary folder. She wrote a simple message to her mother and put it in her bag, ready to post in Malaga. She wanted to send one from every port. That way she wouldn't feel so guilty about leaving her to come away on the cruise. And now she intended to take her time and have a good look round the shops. She had nothing to do, and all day to do it in, she told herself.

David Anderson had also decided to look round the shops. Almost immediately he saw Susie Cunningham. This was his chance and he took it. Apparently not looking her way, he moved into her path and brushed against her. Then quickly holding her arm as if to steady her, he apologized. 'I'm so sorry. Please forgive me.'

'That's all right. No harm done.' She realized who it was: The man who reminded her of Paul, and she felt odd.

'Do forgive me.' He then pretended surprise and said, 'I've seen you somewhere before. Aren't you a photographer?'

Susie was taken aback by his question. It was the same one that Mark Sutherland had used when he spoke to her during their brief meeting. She was intrigued as to why he was asking the same question. 'Yes. But how did you know?'

He acted his answer with perfect timing. 'This is really amazing. I was with a friend for just a few moments and you were taking photographs. You wouldn't have seen me. You were too busy doing your job.'

She became inquisitive. 'Where was this?'

'I'm trying to think … What were you photographing? The chap I was with only called in to see this man for just a minute or so and while they were chatting I kept looking at the lovely photographer. I remember thinking to myself, you should have been on the other side of the camera.'

Flattered, she said, 'Well, thank you. But exactly when and where was this?'

Pretending to think, he said, 'Only recently. Now where the devil was it?'

'Was I photographing models?' Susie asked. 'I just recently did a shoot for Paul Anderson Promotions. He runs a model agency in Chelsea. Could that have been it?'

'Of course! That's where it was, a flat in a large block. That was it. Look, we can't very well talk here. Fancy a cup of coffee?'

She was curious and wanted to know more about this man. 'That would be nice, thank you.'

They went to the coffee bar and found a quiet corner to sit. David got the coffees and while he was doing so, Susie kept thinking how much he reminded her of Paul. It was not just his walk and facial similarity that she found disconcerting, it was the way he spoke. She found it rather too coincidental that he mentioned her shoot at Paul's.

David returned with the coffees and sat down. 'My name is David by the way. David Newman. And if I'm not mistaken, you are, no don't tell me. Shirley, no … Susie! Am I right?'

'Yes. But how do you remember my name? Who told you? I suppose it was Paul.'

'Paul?'

'Paul Anderson. The man I was commissioned by. I thought you knew him.'

'My friend knew him. I only met him briefly.'

'And yet he told you my name?' She was getting more and more curious.

'Either him or my friend. Anyway, it doesn't matter who told me. I'm delighted to meet you. Aren't you sharing a table with a gorgeous dark-haired girl?'

'Yes. So she's gorgeous but I'm only lovely. You sure know how to hurt a girl, Mr Newman,' she said with a grin.

'Please call me David.' His friendly smile was another thing that was so similar to Paul. 'And I'm Susie. But then you know that. I'm really very flattered that you remember me.'

'You know what they say. Once seen, never forgotten. Tell me about this Paul. Do you know him well?'

'Why do you ask?' She felt slightly awkward.

'Just wondered what a man who has models all over his flat is like, that's all.'

'I don't think he has them there all the time. That was a special occasion. Just for the shoot. Although I imagine he never runs short of female company.'

'He must have chatted you up, surely?'

'What makes you say that?' She felt awkward again.

He could see that talking of Paul disturbed her and began digging deeper. 'Well, to be honest, if you came to work for me, I'd certainly try and chat you up. So did Paul?'

'Why do you keep on about a man you say you only met for a brief moment?'

'Because in that short time, I got the feeling that he wasn't a very nice man. Am I right?'

Susie was fascinated by his assessment of Paul. 'What was it about him that makes you say that?'

'I don't know. Male intuition I suppose. I had the feeling that he perhaps used his model agency for something a little more devious.' Her reaction told him that he was hitting a raw nerve.

'How strange that you should say that,' she said slowly. 'I had begun to get the same feeling.'

'To be honest with you, Susie, from what I was told about him by my friend, and from my own vibes, I think Mr Paul Anderson was a kinky, shady character, not to be trusted.' David had made a slip by saying *was* and hoped she wouldn't pick it up. He decided to quickly try and cover his faux pas. 'Right now he's probably up to no good.'

'You could be right. To be honest, it was a while before I actually started doubting him. He's a very charming man when he wants to be. And an extremely plausible liar, I'm afraid.'

'When did you last see him?' He made the question sound innocent.

'Not for a while. You're right about him being devious. He rang me last Saturday and invited me to dinner. I decided to go and see him as I needed to talk to him, but I arrived to find that he'd gone out anyway. So if I really had gone and expected to have dinner I could have starved.'

Thoughtfully she added, 'It was strange that. But I shall make a point of contacting him when I get back. There are a few things I've got to sort out with Mr Anderson.'

David began to wonder about Susie Cunningham. Either she was a good actress, or she really had no idea that Paul was dead. At the moment he wasn't sure which.

Susie wanted to get off the subject of Paul. 'What do you do for a living, David?'

'I run an office cleaning business near Sevenoaks in Kent. Nothing as exciting as photographing models, I'm afraid.' He found the words easy to say and was very convincing.

'Let me tell you that photographing models can be bloody hard and boring. Getting them to stay in one position while you shoot can be a pain, I promise you.'

David saw his chance to switch the discussion back to Paul and light-heartedly said, 'Perhaps the reason you couldn't get a reply from this Paul on Saturday, was because someone had shot him.'

'That's a terrible thing to say!'

'You're right. It was a bad joke. Let's change the subject and talk about tomorrow. Have you any plans?'

'I'm going out with my fiancé.' She smiled. 'So if you were going to chat me up, sorry.'

For some reason he hadn't expected her to be travelling with anyone. 'Fiancé? Not the handsome devil that sits next to you and my dark-haired beauty?' he asked her.

'That's the one.' The thought of James made her face light up.

'All right, I believe you.' He gave her a warm smile. 'What a pity you're engaged. I really would like to—'

'Chat me up? I thought you were already. Now Carol

would be a challenge for you. I doubt if any man has been able to get her to be serious for more that five minutes.'

'Oh all right.' He pretended hurt. 'If it has to be Carol, I accept the challenge. Will you introduce me?'

'But I thought you would have done that yourself during that minute of ecstasy in the lift.' She spoke with a gentle sarcasm.

David couldn't help being amused by her and although it would mean that his dream of interviewing a killer and making money with his story would suddenly end, he was beginning to like Susie Cunningham. 'We didn't have time to do much talking, I'm afraid. We were too busy getting ecstatic.' They laughed and were starting to relax with each other.

'If you really want to meet Carol properly I shall probably see her for a drink before lunch. Why don't you come along and I can introduce you to her, properly?'

'Great. Thank you.'

'Don't thank me, David. I warn you that Carol isn't like any woman you've met before. She will probably embarrass you something rotten.'

'Challenge accepted. Will your chap be there?'

'No. Poor darling's in bed with some sort of bug. That's just reminded me, I'd better get back to my cabin in case he phones.'

'I'm sorry to hear that he's ill. Has he seen a doctor?'

'Oh yes.' She refrained from laughing. 'He certainly has.'

'What about tomorrow? Will he be well by then? Because if he isn't I'd be only too pleased to be your companion. I'd bring my girlfriend as a chaperone.'

'Your girlfriend? I thought you were alone.'

'She chatted me up a short while ago and she's won me over completely. You'll see her at lunch, sitting next to me. A wonderful lady of eighty-something.' He held his hand to his heart and sighed.

Susie laughed and got up to go. 'It's very kind of you but if James is still unwell tomorrow, I shall probably just go for a short stroll and come back on board. I'll see you at the Neptune bar around noon though and introduce you to you know who. Goodbye. And thanks for the coffee.'

'Goodbye for now.' David was fascinated by her openness and lovely personality. The idea of her being capable of killing his brother was now becoming ridiculous. She seemed to be a very nice person and he had become attracted to her in the short time he had been in her company. His only regret was that she was engaged. But never mind, he thought, Carol, the lady of the lift, sounded interesting and he looked forward to meeting her in more seductive surroundings.

When his contact at Chelsea Police station informed him of Geoffrey Harper's death, Erik de Jager's anxiety intensified. He was a very careful man and liked his business dealings to run as smoothly as possible. Everything seemed to be going well until the death of Paul Anderson. He was beginning to wish that he had not started this recent operation. The only good thing was that nothing could link his name with the venture. Providing there were no snags with the exchange in Piraeus, he would be able to relax. As long as his associate on the ship could be trusted to carry out his task, there would be no problem.

He sat looking at the view from his luxury home and began to wonder what his wealthy and influential neighbours would think if they knew of his involvement with narcotics. Here was Erik de Jager, making a fortune because people craved the pleasures that he could supply for them. But Mr de Jager had sold the main import to his dealer, he didn't care who ruined their bodies by using it. After all, he told himself, if he didn't import it, somebody else would.

Sergeant Marsh waited patiently while Mr Lucas studied the photographs of the male models. One by one he discarded them until he had seen them all.

'I'm sorry, sergeant. I cannot say whether or not any of these men were here last Saturday. You must understand that unless I actually see a visitor with one of the residents, I have no idea who is visiting whom.'

'Yes, I quite understand that, sir. It was just that we felt one of these men might have called on Mr Anderson and that you would remember seeing them if they had.'

'I'm sorry I cannot be of more help.' He handed the photo file back. 'Tell me. Did you find that young lady?'

'Miss Cunningham? I'm afraid we still have no idea where she is at the moment. But we will find her eventually.'

'And what about the young man?'

'Oh yes, we found Mr Harper but he wasn't able to help us I'm afraid.' He didn't want to go into any details and upset the old gentleman. 'Well, I'll be off now. Thank you again for your help, sir.'

Mr Lucas gave a despondent sigh. 'I've not been much help at all. I'm sorry, sergeant.'

Dick Marsh shook hands with him and left. He had never thought the old man would recognize any of the models but at least he had done a bit more leg work while he imagined Inspector Forward was relaxing with a drink somewhere.

He was taking a short cut to the King's Road when he passed Bellingdon Avenue which suddenly rang a bell. He stopped the car and tried to remember where that name had cropped up recently. Then it suddenly came to him. Harper's ex-boyfriend, Stephen Conley, lived in Bellingdon Avenue. Believing in fate, Dick Marsh reversed and stopped on the corner. He took out his notebook, found Conley's number and rang it. Conley was in and gave his address as number seventeen, flat two.

Stephen Conley was a slim, good-looking young man in his mid-twenties. Blond highlights gave his neatly cut hair a Scandinavian look. His flat was tastefully furnished, spotlessly clean, and obviously owned by a fastidious person. Accepting Conley's invitation to sit on the cream leather sofa, Sergeant Marsh was about to speak when Conley asked with anxious concern, 'Have they caught him?'

'Caught who, sir?'

'The bastard who killed Julian.'

'Not yet, I'm afraid. But we aren't dealing with that case, sir. Wandsworth CID are in charge of that one.'

'Then why are you here, sergeant?' His question was terse.

Dick Marsh wasn't sure himself, but couldn't tell the man that he was just passing and acted on impulse. 'I just wondered if you might have had any further thought regarding the Paul Anderson murder, sir. When I spoke to you on the phone I got the impression that you were glad he was dead. Was I right?'

Conley showed no emotion at all as he answered, 'Yes.'

His honesty surprised the sergeant. 'Why exactly? What was it about Mr Anderson that you disliked so much?'

Conley hesitated for a moment, then began his barrage of abuse. 'He was a jumped-up, self-opinionated, evil bastard who cared only about one person, himself. Oh, I know that I worked for him but that was only because I needed to get the better jobs, and Paul Anderson was getting in with some of the top magazines, which meant bigger money. In this game we have only a few years to make the big time. You know the old song: "Nobody wants a fairy when she's forty". Well, it's true I'm afraid. When I joined the Anderson team, Julian and I had been together just over a year.' He started to sound tearful. 'Then I made the fatal mistake of introducing him to that bastard, Anderson.'

'Was Geoffrey Harper ever one of his clients?'

'Good God no! If Julian had ever wanted to model he most certainly wouldn't have been a client of Anderson's.'

'Why was that?'

'Because Julian was the most wonderful man you have ever seen. He would have been with the finest management in the world.' Then with contempt, he added, 'Not that prat, Anderson.'

'I don't quite understand. If he could have been such a success as a model, why wasn't he one?'

'Julian didn't like or need the world of modelling. He had no time for it. Especially the idea of posing near naked. Always said it was a cheap way to earn a living.' He began fighting back the tears again. 'He had a good life. And he would be enjoying it now if he had stayed with me. But he loved adventure. He liked taking risks.

And when he met Paul he found him exciting. Paul talked Julian into some sort of venture that appealed to his sense of daring.'

'What exactly was the venture. Do you know?'

'I never had any idea. Julian refused tell me. But knowing that cunning Anderson brain it would have been something I would never have approved of. Something risky and illegal, I could take bets on that.' He began to recover his composure and asked, 'Would you like a coffee?'

'No thank you, sir. I shall have to leave in a few moments. Knowing these men as you did, do you think it possible that Mr Harper could have killed Anderson?'

Conley didn't hesitate in his reply. 'Oh yes. Anyone who knew Paul could have happily killed the bastard.'

'And do you believe that Mr Harper actually did?'

Conley sat shaking his head. 'I don't know. I really don't.'

'Then he was capable of doing so?'

'Julian was a gentle and wonderful person. But he was a man who stood his ground. Physically, he wouldn't be afraid of anyone, and God help any fool who really upset him and tried to get the better of him.'

Dick Marsh decided to play a hunch. 'We had hoped that his diary might shed some light on his death.'

The surprise on Conley's face was exactly what Marsh had expected. 'Diary? What diary?'

'The one they found at his home.'

'Julian never kept a diary. No, sergeant, if you found a diary I can assure you it wasn't his.'

'He didn't have a friend named Roger who was HIV positive?'

Conley looked stunned. 'That's Barry's friend!'

The sergeant raised an eyebrow. 'Barry? Who's Barry?'

'The man who shares this flat with me.' He was getting a bit edgy. 'He and Roger used to live together.'

Sergeant Marsh felt that he was on to something. 'And does Barry keep a diary?'

'Yes. But there must be a simple explanation.'

'Where is Barry now?

'Away. His note just said that he'd been called away and would be in touch. I assumed it was a family matter. His mother's been ill, you see.'

Conley was becoming agitated and Sergeant Marsh felt that he was getting somewhere at last. 'When did he leave, sir?'

'His note was dated Saturday.'

'And you haven't been in contact with him at all?'

'No.' Conley became pale.

'Then would you mind telephoning and finding out if he is actually there at his mother's?'

'You don't think something has happened to him, do you? If you've got his diary. If it *is* his. I mean ...' He anxiously looked among pieces of paper by the phone. 'I know it's here somewhere ... Here it is!' He dialled and waited nervously for a reply. 'Hello. Is that you, Marion? ... It's Stephen ... Fine thanks ... How's your mother? ... Oh good ... Is Barry there? ... Well when did he leave? ... He hasn't? ... But I thought he was with you ... Well, when did you see him last? ... No. No. I must have misunderstood.' He began trembling. 'Say hello to your mother ... I will. Bye.' He hung up and looked totally confused. 'They haven't seen him. So where is he?'

Sergeant Marsh tried not to upset Conley any more than

he had to and casually said, 'I wonder if you could give me a description of Barry, sir, then we can check that he hasn't been involved in an accident.'

'Yes, of course. Medium height. Dark hair. Brown eyes. Very good-looking. Probably wearing a polo neck sweater and a bomber jacket. Oh God, I hope nothing's happened to him.'

'This description you've given me would almost fit that of Geoffrey Harper.'

'Barry's a lot like Julian. I think that's why I became so attracted to him.' He became distraught. 'I couldn't bear it if something's happened to Barry as well.'

'I'm sorry to ask this, sir, but have you any idea who it was who killed Mr Harper?'

Suddenly, Conley burst into tears and Dick Marsh wished he hadn't asked the question. He had never seen a man cry like Conley. He felt embarrassed and wasn't sure what to do next. If it had been a woman he could have offered a handkerchief or a shoulder to cry on. But Sergeant Marsh didn't feel inclined to either option in this case. He simply sat, waiting for Conley to get himself together.

With a final heavy sniff, Conley wiped his eyes and nose, then apologized for his behaviour. 'Sorry about that. It was silly of me. In answer to your question, no, I have no idea who would want to harm Julian.'

Dick Marsh got to his feet. 'Of course. Thank you for your time.' He followed Stephen Conley to the front door. As he was about to leave he asked, 'Oh, just one other thing, sir. You referred to Mr Harper as Julian and not by his real name, Geoffrey. Why is that?'

'As I told you when you telephoned, he never used the

name Geoffrey. He hated it and always preferred Julian. It was the name everyone knew him by.'

Sergeant Marsh smiled and said, 'Of course, I remember now. Well, thank you again, sir.'

He walked to his car feeling sure there was more to be discovered. But after seeing Conley cry, he didn't feel that he could go through that experience again in a hurry.

CHAPTER NINE

The sun deck was packed with people as Susie looked for Carol, who was sitting on a sun bed and wearing a large sun hat. Carol was engrossed in her book, but sensing someone approaching her she looked up and smiled at her visitor. 'Susie! Don't tell me you've decided to sunbathe?'

'No thanks. I came to see if you were still OK for a drink before lunch.'

'Oh, what a shame. I've been invited to the officers' ward room. Do you mind?'

'That's a pity. I had a date lined up for you. I shall just have to suffer having him all to myself,' said Susie with a deep sigh.

Carol became instantly interested. 'Who is he?' Susie gave a cheeky smile. 'So, while James is in his sick bed you've got a bit on the side!'

'Carol! It's you whom this man wants to meet. He's the lift man.'

Carol threw an upward glance of despair. 'Oh God. Not him.'

'Yes, him.'

'If it's a choice between him and a ship's officer then it's no contest. In fact, as I'm in a generous mood, I shall let you have him all to yourself. You lucky girl.'

'It's a shame you don't like him. He thinks that you're the cat's whiskers.'

'The next time I see him, remind me to meow.' Looking at her watch she made a move. 'I must put on a fresh face before I go to the ward room. Funny they call it a "ward" room.' Then, with a twinkle in her eye, she said, 'I wonder if it's like a hospital ward, with beds. That could be jolly.'

Susie gave her a reprimanding look. 'You're incorrigible.'

'I know. Have fun with the lift boy. Ciao.'

As Carol walked away, Susie checked her watch and realized that she just had time to call James before her date with David. As she was hurrying back to her cabin, an announcement came over the ship's public address system. It was asking for Mr David Anderson of cabin F36 to contact the main reception desk. When she heard the name it made her think of Paul and then she recalled that Paul had a brother David, and thought what a coincidence it was that someone of that name was on board. Then something else came to mind that disturbed her. It was the first impression she'd had when she saw David Newman – the way some of his characteristics had reminded her of Paul. Although she had never seen the brother, the thought went through her mind how strange it was that she was meeting a man named David who was so like the one person she wanted to forget. She arrived at the cabin and made the call to James.

He was on his way back to the police station when it came to him what he should have asked Stephen Conley before he left, and DS Marsh had no intention of facing his inspector until he'd done what he should have done. He turned the car around and drove back to Conley's place, hoping that he hadn't gone out. The last thing he wanted was to hear his superior calling him a bloody fool for not thinking of it immediately. But it was exactly what he was calling himself at that moment.

Susie was waiting for David and as it had gone midday, she thought it was odd that he wasn't there. He had been so keen to meet Carol properly and yet appeared to have changed his mind. Or had Susie's description of her frightened him off? She decided to give him a few more minutes before leaving, and was debating whether or not to order herself a drink, when she saw David hurrying towards her. He was out of breath and obviously pleased to see that she was still there.

'Sorry. I thought you might have given me up.' He sat down and gave a sigh of relief. 'Phew. What a panic.'

'Is something the matter?'

'Not really, no. It's just that they decided to upgrade my cabin but left it to the last minute to inform me. I've been moving from one deck to another. Anyway, it's done now.' He gave her a smile. 'What can I get you?'

'I think I'd like a gin and tonic, please.'

'I'll have a large scotch. I think I need one.' He looked round for a steward. 'It will be quicker if I get them. I won't be a minute.'

As he went to the bar, Susie remembered the call for David Anderson and wondered if there actually was any connection. She watched him as he ordered and the similarity to Paul was even more pronounced. She tried to tell herself that it was just her imagination but as he walked back towards her, she had a strange, uncomfortable feeling.

David sat down and looked at his watch. 'Where's the lovely Carol?'

'She won't be coming.' Susie tried to look casual. 'Carol had a previous engagement that I didn't know about. Sorry.'

'Don't be sorry. I'm happy to be alone with you.'

She could hear Paul saying the same words in the same way and her curiosity made her pursue the subject of his cabin. 'So, what's the new cabin like?'

'Great.' He had a contented look about him. 'It's actually got a window with real daylight coming in. Unlike the dark cupboard I had before.'

'What deck was that on?' she tried to sound casual.

'F deck. Now I'm in C109. You'll have to let me show it to you some time. Cheers.'

She acknowledged him by raising her glass and sipped her gin and tonic. As she watched him, he appeared self-confident with no apparent interest in Carol any more. To Susie, it was exactly like being with Paul again. Full of self-importance, and with a hint of conceit in his manner.

Susie remembered that the announcement was for the person in cabin F36 and was sure that David Anderson was sitting next to her now. She wasn't frightened but curious as to what the man was up to. Why had he made up the story of meeting her with one of his friends? And if he was Paul's brother, why didn't he say so? She wished Carol was there right now to give her the moral support she needed.

'How's your boyfriend?' His question broke her thoughts.

'He's a lot better. In fact he's hoping to be OK for dinner tonight,' she said, trying to behave normally.

'Damn!'

'What's wrong?'

He gave a boyish grin. 'That means I won't be able to take you out on the town tomorrow.'

There was a nervous relief in her laugh. 'Oh, I see. Sorry about that but you know what these fiancés are like. They're not too keen on sharing their girls with other men. So what was so wrong with cabin F36, David?' She was determined to find out the truth about this man.

'It was literally a cupboard with ...' he was caught off guard by her question. 'What made you think it was F36?' His effort to appear innocent wasn't working and he knew it.

'Because I heard them call you to the reception desk. As a matter of fact, everyone on the ship heard them call for Mr David Anderson of cabin F36.' She was trembling inside. More with anger than fear, and a feeling of satisfaction that she had the courage to face up to his deception.

He knew he wasn't fooling her any more and threw up his hands in a gesture of surrender. 'I give up.'

'Well, would you kindly tell me what the hell you thought you were playing at? Did Paul put you up to this, to keep an eye on me? Because for your information, Mr Anderson, I don't belong to your brother. I was just a stupid woman who thought she could earn a living in this world and, heaven forgive me, I fell for his charm and flattery. It appears that you Anderson boys both think you're God's gift to women. Well, you aren't!' She found it difficult to appear calm in such a public place as her breathing increased with her anger.

David's mood became more conciliatory towards her and he sounded sincere as he said, 'Comparing me with Paul is just about the worst insult anyone could throw at me. You see, I happen to think that my brother was a first-class shit.'

By the way that he spoke, Susie believed he meant it and was surprised. 'I agree with you entirely. And when you get home you must inform him of the fact. I shall certainly be letting him know where I stand. I may not be quite as explicit as you, but I'm sure he'll get the message. In fact I intended to put my feelings on the line before I came away, but your dear brother wasn't there when I called, despite having invited me to dinner. As you so eloquently said, he's a first-class shit.' She thought for a moment, then asked, 'So why *are* you on this ship?'

His gentle laugh was that of defeat. 'I came looking for you, Miss Cunningham.'

'I'm serious, David.'

'So am I.'

She looked at him with suspicion as she said, 'I don't understand.'

'I believe you. You really don't know, do you?'

She began showing her frustration. 'Know what?'

'When did you go to see Paul?'

'Saturday evening. But I didn't see him because he wasn't there. I just told you that.'

'Oh, he was there all right.'

'Then why didn't he answer?'

'He couldn't. Because when you called to see him, he was dead.'

It was obvious to him by the look on her face that Susie

knew nothing of his brother's death. She was shocked and unable to take it in at first. 'Dead? If this is your idea of a joke, it isn't funny.'

'It's true. His cleaning lady found his body when she went in on Sunday morning.'

'Good God, you're serious.'

'Yes I am. Very serious. Paul died on Saturday evening at around 7.30 according to the police.'

Suddenly she was overcome with remorse. 'And there I was, cursing him for not being there. Hell, I feel awful. I must have been there just after it happened. What was it, his heart?'

David saw no reason to be delicate about it any more. 'No. Somebody killed him. He was murdered.'

'Murdered!' She picked up her drink and finished it. 'How do you mean, murdered?'

'According to the police, he was beaten over the head.' He saw that she was losing her colour. 'Let me get you another drink.'

He emptied his own glass and went to the bar to reorder, leaving Susie staring at the floor in a mild state of shock. David returned to her and put the glass into her hand. She had a quick drink as she tried coming to terms with the dreadful news.

'Who could have done such a thing? Do the police know who it was?'

'They have two suspects, I understand.' He wasn't prepared to go into details as to who they were at that moment.

Susie was very confused as she said, 'I know it may sound silly, but why aren't you in London? There must be things to sort out. Shouldn't you be there?'

'I've done all I can for the time being.'

'But I still don't understand why you're on this ship.'

'Let's just say that I had a hunch I should come away after Paul's death, and this was the one ship that had a cabin going spare. Call it fate that you were on it as well.' He gave her a warm smile.

She found herself torn between liking and hating him. 'You certainly are a difficult man to fathom.'

'Like Paul, you mean?'

'Yes. Just like Paul.' She finished her drink and stood up to leave. 'If you don't mind, I'll go now. I'd like to have a rest for a while and get over this awful news.'

'Aren't you having lunch?'

'I think I'll give lunch a miss today. Thank you for the drinks. Oh, and I don't want to mention anything about Paul to anyone. Not yet anyway. I'd be grateful if you didn't say anything in front of James, or my table companions. It might upset their holiday and I don't want James worrying now that he's beginning to feel better.'

'You have my word.'

'Thank you.'

She left the table and walked out of the bar, leaving him thinking what a fool he had been with his dream of making a fortune from an exclusive interview with a killer. If there was one thing of which David was convinced, it was that Susie Cunningham knew nothing of his brother's murder until he had informed her of it. Either that, or Susie was an extremely clever and devious lady. He ordered another drink and decided to enjoy the cruise now that he had paid for it. His only regret was that he wouldn't have a good story to sell to the national papers after all.

*

When Sergeant Marsh arrived back at the police station, he was feeling pleased with his morning's work. Bill Forward was on the phone to Lewis Madison as he walked into the office.

'That's all right, Mr Madison. I said we would let you know when we had confirmation of Geoffrey Harper's death and … Oh, could you hold on a minute, sir?' Sergeant Marsh was waving to his inspector, signalling that he should stop the conversation with Madison. Forward was curious to say the least as he continued, 'Sorry, sir. Something important just came up. Could I ring you back? Thank you, sir.' He hung up and looked at Marsh. 'Do you mind telling me what all that gesticulating was about?'

'Sorry, but I think you should hear where I've been and what I managed to learn, before confirming anything about Harper being dead.'

Bill Forward sat waiting. 'Go on. Tell me.'

Dick Marsh gave a quick account of his interview with Lucas and Conley. And how he returned to correct his earlier oversight.

'Luckily, Conley was still there when I got back to the flat. That's when I asked for the piece of paper that his friend Barry had written his message on. And this is it.'

The inspector looked at it. 'Good work, sunshine. Get that diary over here.'

Sergeant Marsh was opening the filing cabinet when he said, 'Can I ask you a favour, sir?'

'Of course. What is it?'

'Could you stop calling me *sunshine*? It sounds like one

of those breakfast drinks.' He took the diary from the drawer.

'What do you want me to call you then?'

'Either sergeant, or by my first name.'

Bill Forward smiled to himself. 'If you'd rather be called Dick, so be it. But I think I'd rather be a Richard than a Dick, sunshine. Now let's have a look here.' He turned to the first pages of the diary and compared the writing with that on the note paper, while Dick Marsh sat, realizing that he would probably remain 'sunshine' for ever with his new boss.

'Well, I don't need a hand-writing expert to tell me that this is the same writing. So now we know that this isn't our friend Harper's diary. In fact, it's on the cards that this Barry's disappearance is more serious than Conley realizes,' said Bill.

'That's what I thought,' said Marsh. 'Suppose the body they found in the lake was this Barry, not Harper? That would suggest that our Geoffrey is still alive. Which is what we believed right at the start. And there's something else.' He took a clear plastic bag from his pocket, in which was a small bedside alarm clock.

'What's that?'

'Barry Summers' alarm clock. It will have his prints on it and they can compare them with the man they found in the lake at Wimbledon.'

Bill Forward was impressed. 'You have been a busy boy. Good work, sunshine.'

Dick Marsh was happy to forgo being called by his preferred Christian name in return for the praise he was receiving.

'Get that clock to the forensic boys and I'll call Mike

Dawson and let him know what's happening. Oh, and by the way, thanks for letting me know that this Barry's name is Summers.' Then added with sarcasm, 'Nice of you to share that bit of information with me.'

Sergeant Marsh picked up the bag containing the clock and left the office without replying. He couldn't help wondering why, after getting praise for his work, his inspector then had to put him down over Barry Summers' surname. Then he began to wonder if he would ever treat a sergeant like that, assuming that he got promoted to inspector. After giving the matter careful thought, he knew that he probably would. But of one thing he was certain. He would never call his subordinate 'sunshine'.

As he walked to the forensic department, he was still feeling annoyed about his superior's put-down regarding Summers' surname. Then suddenly, another thought occurred to him. He wondered if the name Cunningham was actually that of Susie's natural father. Or perhaps it was her mother's maiden name, or just a pseudonym she used for professional purposes. He knew that if it was either of the latter two, it would explain why the lady seemed to have vanished, and why immigration would have no knowledge of her having left the country because the name in her passport would be different. He decided not to say anything to his inspector, until he had made one or two phone calls.

When Kenneth Dunwoody went looking for his wife, he was delighted to see her sitting in a sun bed next to the lovely dark-haired young woman he'd seen with Susie Cunningham in the dining room. 'Ah, there you are Sheila. Found a lady to talk to?'

Sheila smiled and said to Carol. 'This is my husband I was telling you about.'

Kenneth stood to attention and half-joking, gave a salute. 'Major Kenneth Dunwoody. Retired. At your service.'

Carol pretended to be impressed as she said, 'Well. That's the first time I've been offered service from a real live major. I'm Carol Mason. Your wife and I were just getting to know each other, Kenneth.'

'Good show. Sorry to interrupt your chinwag, ladies. Looking for somewhere to sit but all the sun beds seem to be occupied.'

Sheila looked at her watch. 'You can have mine, Kenneth. I've got to go for my manicure. See you later, Carol. Don't let him bore you with army talk.'

'Thanks for your company,' said Carol as Sheila left.

'I'll certainly try not to bore you, Carol. If I do, just tell me to shut up,' said Kenneth as he sat on the edge of the sun bed. 'I must say I'm delighted to meet you. Always admired you across the dining room. Not often one sees beautiful women like you.'

'Oh, I'm sure you've had your share of beautiful women. I imagine you looked incredibly handsome in your uniform and drove a few poor women wild,' she said flatteringly.

Kenneth gave a warm smile. 'Pity I haven't got my old uniform here. Like to think your assumption is still correct.'

'Why Kenneth, are you saying you'd like to drive *me* wild?' she whispered, goading him on.

'By jove, yes,' he said breathlessly.

'What makes you think you need a uniform to do that?'

she said, enjoying the fact that she was getting him sexually excited. 'I think we'd better leave before we regret this naughty conversation.' She smiled.

'If I was a younger man it might not be just the conversation that got naughty,' he whispered, giving her a wink.

'I imagine you could get *very* naughty without being a younger man, Kenneth,' she said provocatively.

'We must continue this at a more convenient time, my dear. The sooner the better, eh?'

Carol gave him a warm smile and Kenneth got up and hurriedly made his way off the deck, leaving Carol amused at how easily she was able to arouse him.

Despite the beautiful weather, Susie had stayed in her cabin rather than go up on deck and sit in the fresh air. She was still trying to come to terms with Paul Anderson's death. The thought that while she was trying to get a reply from his doorbell, he was lying inside dead, was making her feel sick. The one person that she wanted to talk to was James, but she still didn't want him to know about her relationship with Paul. She couldn't bear the thought of losing James. Not now.

She wished that she had never set eyes on Paul. She felt that his influence over her had been nothing but bad. And now there was his brother. What had really made him come on this particular ship? she wondered. And why did she feel that there was something he wasn't being honest about? Her mind was confused and she was finding it difficult to make sense of all these problems that had suddenly arisen. There was only one thing that she was certain of: her life would have been a lot happier if she had never met Paul Anderson. Susie closed her eyes and tried to rest. She wanted to look her normal self when she saw James again, and not give him any cause for concern.

She had fallen asleep when the sound of the phone ringing woke her. She lifted the receiver and heard a very quiet, sexy male voice. 'Is that the gorgeous lady whom I can't wait to be alone with?'

'I hope so,' she whispered, mimicking his voice. 'And is that the man who makes me feel so special?'

'I could make you feel more than special if you'll let me.'

'Oh yes, please.'

'I wish I was there now, looking at you in your underwear.'

'Do you?' Susie asked, wondering why James was talking this way. 'What do you mean?'

'I could remove it slowly, piece by piece and give you a time you will never forget.'

Susie was suddenly embarrassed and spoke in her normal voice. 'I think this conversation is getting silly, don't, you James?'

The male voice suddenly changed from quiet and sexy as he said, 'Oh God! Sorry. Sorry,' then quickly hung up.

As soon as he put down the receiver she realized it wasn't a silly call from James and wondered which woman the man had believed he was talking to.

Lionel and Sybil had eaten entirely alone and wondered where the others had got to. They left the restaurant and were making their way towards D deck when Sybil decided to call at the photographers and leave a film to be developed. Lionel went on to the cabin alone.

He took the stairs instead of the lift and as he arrived on

D deck saw a young man leave Carol Mason's cabin and go hurrying off to the stairway at the opposite end of the long corridor. Although the young man hadn't seen him, the reverend could tell that he was young and athletic. Lionel shook his head disapprovingly and wondered how many more young men would be familiar with Carol Mason and the interior of her cabin by the end of the cruise.

He went quickly to his cabin and decided to keep the knowledge of Carol's young man to himself.

Erik de Jager's associate on board the *Verna Castle* was in a jubilant mood. After weeks of careful planning he was only days away from completing the transaction. He would meet Dimitri Leonis at the Milos hotel to make the exchange. But that is where a change of plan would take place. Once he was in possession of the package, the unsuspecting Greek would go into a deep sleep and by the time he woke up, de Jager's associate would have completely disappeared. Even the package he had removed from Paul Anderson's suitcase would never be seen again. The thought of the trusting de Jager being cheated by the one person he relied on, was a source of great amusement to him.

He had arranged his change of identity some months before and was convinced that he would never be found, no matter how much money or time the clever Dutchman spent searching for him. He was now able to gain access to all the cabins and the baggage room. His very convincing impersonation of a crew member had admitted him to the accommodation office for the few moments he needed to obtain a copy of the plastic master key, which was one of four in an unlocked wall cabinet. He had carefully timed its removal from the office while the junior officer on duty was busy issuing instructions to a group of cabin stewards. It was obvious that the key had not been missed, as he had used it occasionally to open his own cabin door and satisfy himself that the electronic code on the pass keys had not been changed.

He poured himself a drink and was thinking how lucky he had been not to be observed in the baggage room when the young steward had entered. He'd been reluctant to hit the boy on the head, but it would have ruined his entire plan had he not done so. And now, Susie Cunningham's leather bag was no longer of any importance, for she would not be taking anything back with her, other than her personal belongings.

He remembered de Jager saying that attractive young women were seldom searched by Her Majesty's customs. But he hadn't considered two other types of people who were never searched: holy sisters of the convent and men of the cloth. The thought of them carrying Erik de Jager's property brought a smile to his face and he poured himself another drink. Just a few more days, he thought, and he could vanish for ever and live in luxury. He had already decided which of the two counterfeit passports he would use, and was completely happy with the plan that he had conceived. It was a plan so perfect that nothing could possibly go wrong. Of that he was convinced.

In the evening James was feeling much better. The long distance phone call he had made also gave him reason to be optimistic. He arranged to meet Susie in their quiet bar and arrived before she did. He ordered a whisky with ice and water and sat at the table he and Susie had occupied on their first visit to that bar. As he sipped his drink, he began thinking of tomorrow and another day ashore with the girl he had fallen madly in love with. He knew that Susie was getting excited about their day in Malaga and hoped that it would not be an anticlimax after their day in Sintra.

He sat watching the passengers walking past the entrance and each time a woman appeared he hoped it would be Susie. He wondered how she would react if she knew about the telephone call he had made. At last she arrived, and he immediately stood up and she hurried into his embrace. As he held her to him he could feel her heart beating quickly. 'Oh, how I've missed you, Miss Cunningham.'

She hugged him and whispered, 'Not as much as I've missed you, doctor.' It was just a brief moment before they found themselves in a passionate kiss. It was a few moments before the sound of someone moving brought them both back to reality. Susie looked around and saw the only other occupant of the bar was leaving. As he walked from his dimly lit corner Susie recognized him. But she waited until he had gone before telling James who the man was. 'That was him!' she said. 'That was the man I told you had stared at me in the shop. The one that hid his face when I was taking pictures on the deck. Either it's my imagination or the man's following me.'

James smiled as he tried to reason with her. 'He was here before we arrived, so he could hardly be following you.'

'Then why did he leave when he saw me just now?'

'Perhaps he thinks you're following *him*!' James

grinned. 'In any case, why would he be following you? Let me get you a gin and tonic.'

She watched him walk over to the bar and tried convincing herself that she was being silly about the man who had left. But she knew something that James didn't. She knew that Paul Anderson had been murdered. That his brother David was now a passenger on board, having conveniently obtained a cabin at the last minute on the same ship that she was on. And she was sure that the man who had just left was watching her. No matter what James thought. She wanted it to just be coincidence that he was on the ship, but since learning of Paul's death she had become edgy. And then she remembered Mark Sutherland, a model she had photographed. A model who also just happened to be on the same ship. Although she believed in chance encounters, there was something about these that made her feel suspicious.

James signed for the drinks and made his way back to their table. As he sat down he raised his glass to her. 'To the future Mrs Kerr. The loveliest lady I know.'

She gave an enquiring look. 'Do I know her?'

'Come to my wedding and you will.' Then he added, 'Better still, come on my honeymoon. Then you'll be certain to.'

Susie was trying to appear calm. 'I accept that offer without condition. How are you really feeling now?'

'Much better. It was just a twenty-four hour bug.'

'You were right to stay in bed. But I did miss you. It was strange not having you there.'

He took her hand and kissed it. Without saying a word they sat, slowly finishing their drinks.

Susie again was thinking of David and the horrible

news he had brought about Paul's murder. She began wondering who could have committed such a terrible crime when she remembered the brown leather bag that was now in James's cabin. Perhaps James had been absolutely right when he suggested she might have been carrying something illegal. Perhaps Paul had lent it so that she would be an innocent courier. The more she thought about it the more nervous she became. If someone on board was involved in one of Paul Anderson's criminal activities, and came looking for the bag, that would put James in a dangerous position. Perhaps the man who had just left the bar was involved. As she began letting her imagination run away with her she saw David come in. Her heart began beating faster again, but this time it was from a fear that he would say something about Paul in front of James. As she tried to appear relaxed David gave a casual wave of acknowledgement and sat at the bar.

'Who is that?' James enquired.

'A man I met briefly this morning.' She tried to sound as natural as possible. 'Apparently he saw me on a photo shoot. I don't remember him but I must have made an impression for him to remember me.'

'Once anyone has seen you they would never forget you, my lovely.' He held up an empty glass. 'Do you fancy another?'

She was glad he accepted her explanation of David without further questioning but wanted to get out of the bar. 'Let's have an early dinner and celebrate your rapid recovery with a nice bottle of wine.' She suggested.

'Why not?'

He got up and she took his arm, holding it tight as they

walked out. Susie decided not to mention the obscene phone call from the man. She didn't want to give James a stupid thing like that to worry about.

CHAPTER TEN

Inspector Forward informed Lewis Madison that there was now some doubt as to whether Geoffrey/Julian Harper was indeed dead. It was now past 6.30 p.m. and he decided to call it a day. Just as he was putting on his coat, Sergeant Tulley from the records department looked in. 'How's the Anderson case shaping up, Bill?' he enquired.

'Don't ask.'

'Bad as that, eh?'

'Worse. I've got three people I need to interview and all of them have vanished into thin air.' He gave the sergeant a brief rundown on the case. They had been colleagues for a long time.

Sergeant Tulley smiled. 'Cheer up. Sounds like you've got a plateful. But no doubt you'll get it sorted. I'd better go. Kathy's got some brochures ready for me to look at. When I retire she's not sure whether she wants to take a holiday villa in France or go on a world cruise. Whichever it is she's determined to spend my retirement pay one way or the other.'

Bill Forward's mouth dropped open. 'A ship! Why the hell didn't I think of that?'

'What are you talking about?'

'Don't you see? Verna Castle could be the name of a ship, not a person!'

'You can soon find out. Look up cruise liners on the net. If you're right, it'll be there. Must go. Good luck.'

As Tulley left, Bill Forward returned to his office and switched on his computer. He sat impatiently waiting for it to boot up. Thanks to a chance remark by his colleague, he believed that he could be getting close to the long-awaited interview with Susie Cunningham. And if his hunch was right, he looked forward to an early start the following morning.

As Sybil and her husband finished their pre-dinner drinks in the Neptune bar, she was curious as to why Lionel had his eyes on every passenger that came and went. 'What is it, dear? Why can't you relax? Are you looking for someone?'

The reverend hesitated. 'Well, yes and no.'

'It must be one or the other. Is it yes or is it no?' She was getting impatient.

Deciding that honesty was the best policy he answered in a low voice, 'If you must know, I was looking for a young man.'

Sybil quickly looked around to see if anyone had overheard, and whispered, 'Keep your voice down! What would people think if they heard such a remark from a man of the cloth?'

'I thought I was keeping my voice down,' he whispered.

'Then explain yourself, Lionel.' She spoke with a fixed smile for the benefit of onlookers. 'What young man are you talking about?'

'I saw a young man leaving Ms Mason's cabin and wondered if I would recognize him again. That's all.'

'I would imagine half the young men on this ship will be wafting in and out of that woman's cabin during the course of this cruise. What was so special about this one?'

'Nothing really. He just seemed so young, that was all.'

Her curiosity grew as she studied every young man in the bar. 'What did he look like?'

'I don't know. I didn't actually see his face.'

Exasperated, Sybil snapped at him. 'Then how do you know who to look for? Come on, let's go in to dinner and do try and act normal. We don't want that Mason woman thinking we're interested in her private life.'

By the time Carol entered the dining room, James and Susie had ordered their meals and were listening to Sybil, who was recommending various churches and cathedrals to visit while they were in Malaga. As Sybil saw Carol the conversation came to an abrupt end. The two men were about to rise but Carol signalled them to remain seated.

'Please don't get up.' She sat and smiled at James. 'I'm so pleased to see that no undertaker is required after all. Are you feeling better now?'

'Thank you, yes. Much better,' James answered politely.

'Good. But you mustn't overdo it, James. You'll be no good to Susie unless you keep your strength up.'

Sybil tried not to show her embarrassment by changing the subject. 'I think you should order dinner. We've all ordered ours.'

Carol picked up her menu and turned to Lionel. 'And what do you recommend, vicar? I am right to call you vicar aren't I? Or would you prefer parson?'

'I really don't mind.' He tried to sound convincing. 'I've

ordered the soup and the loin of pork,' he said with a friendly smile. But when he saw Sybil giving him a reprimanding glare, he turned his attention away from Carol and toyed nervously with his napkin.

'What have you been doing today, Carol?' Susie enquired, in the hope of avoiding an atmosphere. 'Anything exciting?'

'I've been reading the Bible.'

Her reply was received with disbelief. 'If that's true, I hope you've learned something that will improve your way of life,' Sybil said sharply.

'Oh, indeed I have.' Carol sounded reverent. 'As you may be aware, the Roman Catholic church considers divorce a sin.'

Lionel nodded in agreement. 'That is true.'

'And yet, in the Bible it clearly states that if a man is displeased with his wife he should divorce her,' said Carol.

'Ah, you have been reading Deuteronomy 24,' Lionel stated in his ecclesiastic voice. 'But that is in the Old Testament, which the Jewish religion recognizes. But not the Christian church.'

'Oh dear,' Carol sighed. 'Does that mean that you couldn't get rid of your dear wife because you aren't Jewish? How very unfair.'

Sybil was, for once, lost for words.

'Here comes our food,' Susie announced brightly. 'I'm very hungry tonight. Aren't you, Sybil?'

Sybil managed a smile as she replied. 'I was. But I seem to have lost my appetite. In fact, I think I shall just have my soup and nothing else.'

The others were sorry for her and felt embarrassed at

the way Carol had deliberately upset her. They began eating as Carol ordered her prawn cocktail and loin of pork.

The uncomfortable silence was broken by James, who asked Lionel, 'What are your plans for tomorrow?'

'Sybil and I are on the full day tour. It visits some of the beauty spots, including the ruins of a fifteenth-century town that was once the home of Renato Miguel. He was a religious teacher and philosopher you know.'

'Sounds interesting. You must be looking forward to it,' James said, being as friendly as possible.

'Indeed we are,' Lionel confirmed.

As they continued eating, Carol looked around the dining room and noticed David Anderson looking in her direction. She smiled, and was surprised when he suggested, in mime, that she join him for a drink after dinner. Intrigued by his offer, and having nothing better to do, she gave him a nod of acceptance. Then, turning to Susie she gave a sly grin. 'Well, what do you know, my little lift boy has invited me for a drink.'

Susie became uneasy. 'You're kidding!'

'No, really. Do you think I should meow or purr?'

Praying that David would keep his word and not mention anything about Paul's death to her table companions, Susie forced a laugh. 'Because he thinks you're the cat's whiskers, you mean? I'm sure he won't mind as long as you don't try to scratch him.'

'What are you two going on about?' James enquired.

'A young man who can't wait to be alone with me has just played Give Us A Clue across the tables and invited me for a drink. The things he can do with his hands are amazing. If he isn't pushing buttons to make lifts go up, he's inviting girls out for an alcoholic orgy. How could I refuse him?'

James gave a look of despair. 'You really are a one-off Carol.'

'Thank you, darling. I'll pretend that was a compliment.'

Susie smiled at James and said, 'What can you do with her?'

'Oh, don't ask him that. It might embarrass me.' Carol said in an innocent tone.

Although Susie was happy to have James sitting next to her again, she couldn't help worrying about the forthcoming meeting between Carol and David. The idea of Carol learning the true identity of David, or his drinking too much and discussing Susie's affair with Paul Anderson was more than she could bear. All she could do was keep her fingers crossed and hope David would keep his promise to her.

Events later that evening drove all thoughts of David and Carol from Susie's mind. She and James felt so full of love for each other, they made love in Susie's cabin. For the first time in her life, Susie experienced the difference between having sex and making love. And now, with her head resting comfortably on the pillow, her heart was beginning to slow to its normal beat once more.

At first, she was frightened that she might have done the wrong thing by allowing James into her bed. Frightened that it was too soon in their relationship, and the last thing she wanted was to spoil that. But her fears soon disappeared as he held her in his arms and kissed her. She had longed to feel him against her and experience the warmth of his hand as it tenderly explored her sensitive body. Nothing in her wildest fantasies had been as wonderful as the moment she had just experienced with the man she loved.

His arm reached out and pulled her gently towards him once more, and she responded by embracing him. Now there was no question in her mind as to whether she should have allowed him into her bed. She could feel him becoming aroused again and as he began kissing her breasts, she became impatient for him to take her.

Her contented body relaxed once more, and her thoughts of a future with James became more credible. Soon, she began drifting into a deep and satisfying sleep.

It was almost dawn as she slowly woke and reached out to touch her lover. Suddenly, aware that he had gone, she sat up and looked around the cabin. Her eyes went to a note that was on her bedside locker. She took it, and her face lit up as she read:

> Darling,
> I thought I'd better not ruin your reputation so I went to my own bed before the girl brings your morning tea. See you at breakfast.
> I love you.
> James x x

She snuggled down again and cuddled her pillow, wishing it was James that she was holding.

By the time Bill Forward had telephoned the travel agent and discovered the whereabouts of the *Verna Castle*, he had another piece of good fortune. Forensics confirmed that the prints on the alarm clock matched those on the body found in the Queensmere lake on Wimbledon common.

There was no doubt now that it was the body of Barry Summers and not Geoffrey Harper. And just before Sergeant Marsh arrived, he had booked his flight to Malaga and contacted the Spanish police. Then he phoned the solicitor, Madison, and told him the true identity of the body in the lake.

Bill was now able to give the news to his sergeant. 'And you were right about Harper not being the chap found at Wimbledon. His fingerprints matched those on the alarm clock you brought in. Those of Barry Summers.'

'So Harper *is* still alive!'

'Looks that way. And the other good news is I've found Verna Castle.'

'That's great. Where is she?'

'The *Verna Castle* is a bloody cruise ship! That's why no one could find her. It's in Malaga today until 8 p.m., so with a bit of luck I'll be talking to our Miss Cunningham in a few hours. Cunningham is her real name by the way. And as it's on her passport, she must have got through immigration before we put out the all ports warning.'

Sergeant Marsh felt deflated. 'I know it was her real name because I did a check. I didn't know that you had done one as well.'

'If you'd got here earlier you *would* have known, wouldn't you? And, as a young ambitious police officer, I'm surprised you didn't realize the lady we were looking for was a ship.' Before Marsh could answer, he added, 'And even more annoyed that *I* didn't.'

A WPC came in and handed them a copy of the ship's passenger list, faxed through from the travel agency. They quietly scanned it. Bill Forward looked under C. 'Here she is! Cabin B70.'

But Marsh had spotted something else. 'Look here, there's a David Anderson on board as well.'

'Show me!' Bill Forward grabbed the list and looked under A. 'Why didn't I see that?' He was really annoyed with himself. 'It's too much of a coincidence for it not to be Paul Anderson's brother. And you know what this means?'

'That they were both in it together. Him and the Cunningham girl.'

'Looks that way, doesn't it, sunshine? Just for the hell of it, let's see if there's a Geoffrey, Jeremy or Julian Harper on board as well.' He studied the list with Dick Marsh looking over his shoulder. After scrutinizing each name under H they gave up.

'You didn't really expect him to be there as well, did you, guv?'

'No. But it was worth a try. So, Mr David Anderson and the girl are in this together. Now there's a turn up for the book. Come on, let's get our paperwork sorted. It's a two hour flight to Malaga and I want to be there in time for lunch.' He began teasing his sergeant. 'They do a lovely paella in Spain. Beautiful with a glass of their red Rioja. Come on, let's get moving.'

Dick Marsh gave a despondent shake of his head and left the office.

James and Susie had their first breakfast alone, sharing glances and intimate looks until Carol arrived.

'Good morning, lovers. Where are the Mother Superior and her religious mascot this morning?'

'I saw them having breakfast on deck this morning,' Susie informed her. 'I think they fancied something different.'

'Don't we all, darling? And how are you, James? Getting your strength back I hope.'

He found the question amusing but managed a serious reply. 'I'm feeling good as new, thank you. And looking forward to a nice day in Malaga, despite the captain's gloomy forecast of possible showers.'

'Speaking of showers, have you seen that David Newman this morning? My meeting him last night was a big mistake, Susie. Self-opinionated little sod fancied his chances with me, you know.'

'Of course I know. I thought that's why you agreed to have the drink with him,' said Susie.

'Oh, I admit that I was intrigued, but he was just as I thought. A pain in the arse.'

'Was he really that bad?' James enquired.

'Worse. Never mind. Let's have some breakfast and forget last night.' Carol got up to help herself to fruit juice.

A look passed between James and Susie that said they would never want to forget last night.

The steward came and took James and Susie's order for a cooked breakfast. When Carol returned she asked, 'Not having juice or cereal this morning?'

'No. We've chosen a cooked breakfast for a change,' James replied. 'As you told me last night, Carol. I've got to keep my strength up.'

Susie began to blush at his remark, and Carol was quick to notice. She gave a knowing look, and said, 'So I did, darling. I'm glad you took my advice.'

James quickly switched the conversation to the weather and Carol's intention to go shopping. Susie was relieved that David had obviously kept his word and not let Carol know his real identity.

During their breakfast there were constant announcements telling passengers where the gangway was and what tour left from which area of the dockside. By the time they had finished eating it was past 9.30 a.m. and they all left the table, wishing one another a nice day.

James walked Susie to her cabin and as they arrived, the stewardess was there making up the room, so they arranged to meet each other by the gangway in fifteen minutes' time.

Susie told the girl to stay and continue making up the cabin, while she went to the bathroom. After she had finished freshening up, she looked at the third finger of her left hand and imagined her engagement ring adorning it. The ring that James had promised to buy in Malaga. The thought of becoming officially engaged thrilled her and she felt that the day ahead would be one that she would never forget. Susie would certainly remember this day, and before it was over she would experience several emotions, including some that she would not find very pleasant.

CHAPTER ELEVEN

R uth's carer at the Welland Nursing Home in Haslemere had just delivered a postcard to her. It was a photo-graph of an ocean liner from her daughter Susie. The fact that the ship was called *Verna Castle* made her feel obliged to telephone Detective Inspector Forward. When the tele-phone rang it was Sergeant Marsh who picked up the receiver.

'Chelsea Police. Detective Inspector Forward's office.'

'Could I speak to the inspector please?'

'I'm sorry but he isn't here at present. Can I help?'

'He recently came to see a patient of mine at the Welland Nursing Home and asked if she knew a Verna Castle, which she didn't. Well the patient has just received a post-card from her daughter and it's from a ship called the *Verna Castle*. I thought he should know that it was a ship and not a person as he originally thought.'

'It's very kind of you to call, madam. I will pass that information on to the inspector just as soon as I can.'

She felt that she had done her duty and returned to the daily routine of the nursing home.

Dick Marsh looked at his watch, envying his inspector,

who was now on his way to Heathrow Airport to catch the
BA flight to Malaga, due to arrive there at 2.40 p.m. local
time.

The phone rang just as Susie was leaving her cabin and
when she answered it, was surprised to hear David's voice
at the other end. 'Just wanted you to know that you were
right about Carol. She was a real bitch to me last night. I
don't think any man could handle that woman, which is
probably why she's on her own.'

'Sorry your evening didn't work out,' Susie sympa-
thized. 'But I did warn you. Never mind. You might still
meet a nice girl on the ship, who knows.'

'I doubt it. Not many like you on board, I'm afraid.
Should your chap get tired of you, let me know. You've got
my cabin number. Enjoy Malaga.'

'Thank you, David. And thank you for not mentioning
anything about my relationship with your brother.'

'Oh God. I can imagine what a sordid story she would
make of that. Don't worry, I shan't mention it to anyone, so
you can rest easy.'

'Thanks again, David.'

'You're very welcome. Bye for now.'

'Bye.' She hung up, thinking it strange that he made the
comment about James getting tired of her. She left the
cabin and hurried to the gangway. James was already
there and she apologized for keeping him waiting.

'I thought for a moment that you might have run off
with another man,' he joked.

She didn't like him saying it, even in fun. 'I've got the
only man I want.' She held his hand tight. 'He even said he
would buy me a ring today.'

'He did? In that case we'd better find a jeweller before he changes his mind.'

As they walked from the ship she felt happy and couldn't believe that her life had changed so much in the past few days. And all because this man was allocated a place at the same table and chose to sit next to her.

Erik de Jager was surprised when he answered his telephone and heard the voice of his informant. 'I've just heard that the inspector is on his way to Spain to interview the Cunningham girl.'

'So he knows that she's on the ship? Damn! Do you know what time he arrives there?'

'Due there at 2.40 this afternoon, local time. And there's something else.'

'Go on.'

'David Anderson is on board.'

'You mean, the brother?'

'Yes.'

De Jager was puzzled. 'Are you saying that he and the girl are together?'

'He joined the ship in Lisbon. That's all I know. Perhaps your man on board will know what's going on between them.'

De Jager was worried and unable to hide the fact. 'What the hell is he doing there? I don't like it. I don't like it at all. Let me think.' He was trying to make sense of the situation. 'I must contact my colleague on board and warn him. There's something odd about Anderson being on that ship. Very odd indeed. Is there anything else?'

'At the moment, no.'

'If you learn anything else, anything at all, contact me immediately. Immediately, do you hear?'

'Of course.'

Erik de Jager hung up and then dialled the number of the *Verna Castle*, hoping that his colleague had not gone ashore as time was of the essence. He had to know why Anderson had flown to Lisbon and joined the ship that Susie Cunningham was on. Perhaps his colleague on board could find out what the connection was between them. De Jager would not be happy until the mystery of the young man's appearance on the ship had been solved. He got connected to the cabin, keeping his fingers crossed that his associate would answer and know the reason for David Anderson being on board the ship. De Jager was in a nervous state as he waited for an answer to his call.

After clearing immigration Forward was met by Inspector Carlos Mendez, who opened the conversation with polite small talk and then got down to the business in hand as they drove from the airport.

'What exactly do you require of us, Detective Inspector?'

'There are two passengers, both British subjects, on board the *Verna Castle*. I need to talk to them about a murder that took place in London last Saturday. It may be that neither of them are directly involved but at least one of them was seen leaving the premises at which the murder took place. One is a young and very attractive blonde woman.'

Carlos Mendez became interested. 'And the other person?'

'He is the brother of the murder victim. I have learned

that he is to become quite wealthy now that his brother is dead. He may or may not be aware of his good fortune. That is what I intend to find out. But either way, he must have had a good reason to fly out and join the ship in Lisbon, and I would like to know what it was.'

Inspector Mendez agreed. 'I too would be curious.'

Despite the car's air conditioning, Bill Forward removed his jacket. As he did so, Carlos Mendez smiled and instructed his driver to increase the cold air. For the rest of the journey the two men discussed food and drink and became better acquainted.

Although the restaurant that James had taken her to was one of the best in Malaga, Susie was so excited with her beautiful engagement ring that she had lost her appetite. It was a gold band with three diamonds set in platinum, and all through the meal she kept looking at it and moving her hand to watch the light reflecting through stones that had been cut with such precision. The rain that the captain had forecast was falling heavily during their lunch but it didn't have any depressing effect as far as Susie was concerned. All she could think about was showing everyone her new possession, and she intended doing just that at the dinner table.

It was then that she thought of her mother. She wanted so much for her to meet James and was wondering whether she would be able to take in her news. These thoughts were going through her mind as James suddenly asked, 'Is something the matter?'

'I was thinking about my mother.'

'That explains it.'

'Explains what?'

He gently brushed his hand against her cheek. 'The way your mood changed.'

She held his hand. 'Sorry. I just hope that she's having one of her good days when you meet her. I want her to know all about our meeting and that wonderful day in Sintra. It's so dreadful when she cannot comprehend. She was such a happy fun person before she became ill. I wish you had known her then and heard her laughter.'

He hesitated for a moment, then said, 'I wasn't going to say anything until later. And I don't want to build your hopes up too much, but I took the liberty of mentioning your mother to Philip, my partner in the practice. I asked him to check up on both the Welland Nursing Home and Mr Bernard Leddington-White.'

She looked surprised. 'What do you mean, check up?'

'Susie, Philip made a few enquiries and discovered that Leddington-White *owns* the Welland. And it appears that the manager of the home is his mistress. Apparently they've made a fortune over the years by getting private patients into the place.'

'I'm not surprised, the fees that he charges.'

'As a qualified neurologist he specializes in people with memory loss such as Alzheimer's. But Philip heard a rumour that Mr Leddington-White prescribes some patients with drugs that can have a reverse effect. Such as making them mentally confused.'

'But that can't be true, surely?'

'Well if it is, and it can be proved, then Mr Leddington-White could be in serious trouble.'

'Do you mean that all this time he's been keeping my mother on drugs that make her forget things, as if she was suffering from Alzheimer's?'

'As I said, it's just a rumour at the moment.'

'But if it is true, that's a terrible thing to do.'

James was comforting in his reply. 'Philip got the name of your mother's GP from the secretary at the Welland, and has been in touch with him. When Philip told him what he'd heard about Leddington-White's treatment, your mother's GP got her out of the Welland and insisted on knowing what drugs had been prescribed for her. She is now under the care of a neurologist at a clinic in Wimbledon.

Susie tried to absorb what he'd told her but was in a state of shock. 'You mean that my mother is out of that place and in another one where she will get better?'

'No promises. But with the right treatment there's a good chance that she will improve. I expect Philip to telephone me tomorrow to give me a progress report.'

'I still don't understand. Why didn't the nursing staff at the Welland realize what Leddington-White was doing? They must have suspected something surely?'

'We mustn't jump to the conclusion that he acted improperly. If he has, the British Medical Council would come down on him like a ton of bricks. But once her own doctor knew that she was in the Welland, he should have kept an eye on her progress and what medication she was on.'

'He wasn't too happy at my going above his head and putting her in a private clinic, but I couldn't watch her like that and not do something.'

'At least she is now in good hands, so try not to worry.'

Throwing her arms around his neck she said, 'Oh thank you, darling, thank you.'

James held her to him and whispered, 'After all, I want my future mother-in-law fit enough to babysit for us.'

The kiss she gave him was one of loving gratitude and she didn't care about other customers looking at them. After a moment, she composed herself.

James smiled as he said, 'Oh, and I found out who the man is you thought was always staring and following you. The cruise director knows him. He's an eccentric character who comes on every year but hates having his photograph taken; he won't even have one taken with the captain. Apparently, he doesn't like shaking hands with anyone either. He believes it's the way germs are spread from person to person. He likes to eat alone as well.'

Susie frowned. 'I knew he was a bit strange.' Then she said, 'Do you think I could phone my mother? Have you got her new number?'

'Wait till tomorrow, darling. Philip will tell us how she is and whether she can take a telephone call or not. Try and be patient, Susie. Wait just a bit longer.'

After three attempts, Erik de Jager had finally made contact with his colleague on board the ship, and had been able to warn him of Inspector Forward's impending visit. Mr de Jager now felt a lot happier, believing that his package was safe again.

As soon as the phone call had ended, the man de Jager had trusted with his mission, unlocked the security drawer that was built in to all the cabin wardrobes. He then removed the briefcase containing the package he had retrieved from the brown leather bag. He smiled as he imagined Susie Cunningham's reaction if she knew what she had really carried on board. Items that any woman would give her soul to possess. As he checked the contents of the briefcase he began humming to himself. The tune that he chose as he extracted the package was 'Diamonds are a Girl's Best Friend'.

He carefully unwrapped the brown paper parcel and removed from it two small oblong shapes that were sealed in a skin of lead foil to prevent X-ray detection. One of the shapes was quite small in size and even the larger one only measured 15x10x3 centimetres. The smaller one was intended for Dimitri Leonis, while the larger one was to be used to open a bank account in Monaco when the ship called at Monte Carlo. The original plan was for the contents to be taken to a dealer who de Jager had arranged the sale with. Then a bank account was to be opened in the name of Lennox Distributors. Nothing had been left to chance. Even all the papers had been signed to avoid any last-minute problems at the bank. But de Jager's colleague had no intention of opening an account in Monaco, other than for himself.

He took a holdall from the wardrobe and removed a laptop computer from it. When he opened the battery and hard disc compartments they were empty. When he placed both of the packages into the spaces, they fitted perfectly. He was admiring de Jager's planning and ingenuity as he gently closed up the two compartments. De Jager had thought of everything. If anyone were to ask why the processor was not working, he would simply tell them that the battery was flat, and that he was unable to recharge it because he had lost the mains lead. All so very plausible.

His only regret was that he might have to abandon meeting Dimitri Leonis and relieve him of the heroin. But he decided not to be greedy. After all, what would the fifty thousand or so pounds that he would get for the narcotics mean, compared with the two to three million he would get for the diamonds? He was feeling very pleased with himself and gave a self-satisfied chuckle as he thought how easy it was to steal from the great Erik de Jager. So easy. So simple. The whole scam had been so meticulously planned and he was proud of himself. It had been worth all the trouble he'd gone through, and he would soon be an extremely wealthy man.

As David Anderson was walking to his cabin he heard a call put out over the public address system. It was asking for David to contact the purser's office. Curious as to what the purser wanted, he went into his cabin and telephoned. The assistant purser informed him that a gentleman from England wished to speak to him regarding an urgent matter and requested that he went immediately to the office. When he asked who the gentleman was he was shocked to hear the name, Detective Inspector Forward. David put down the phone and hurried to the purser's office.

On the way there, he assumed that it was to do with Paul's death but was puzzled as to how anyone knew that he was on board. And why would the inspector have come all this way unless he had a damned good reason? Then, taking the aft stairway rather than waiting for the lift, he met Carol, who was on her way down to D deck. Seeing that he was flustered, she asked, 'What on earth has happened to the lift boy? You look quite anxious.'

David stopped for a moment. 'As a matter of fact, I'm on my way to meet a VIP.'

'Is my lift boy telling me that he actually knows a VIP?'

'Yes. A Virtuous Inspector of Police.'

'Do be serious.'

'I am being serious. A police inspector from England has turned up and wants to see me. I'll tell you all about it some time. Better not keep him waiting.' He hurried up the stairway, leaving Carol looking very puzzled.

David guessed that it was to do with the fact that he'd known where Susie Cunningham was but hadn't informed the inspector. He became worried and hoped he wouldn't be in too much trouble for withholding evidence.

David was shown into the purser's office and left in the company of Bill Forward and Inspector Mendez. After he was introduced, Carlos Mendez sat in a corner, leaving Inspector Forward to interview David Anderson.

David asked hopefully, 'Have you got him?'

Bill Forward raised an eyebrow. 'Got who, sir?'

'The man who killed my brother of course. Isn't that why you're here?'

'Yes. That is why I am here, sir. But no, so far we haven't been able to apprehend the person who actually committed the crime. Not yet.' Bill Forward watched for any telltale signs of guilt on the face of David Anderson and was prepared to take his time.

David was confused. 'I don't understand. Then why are you here? And how did you know where I was?'

Bill Forward looked and sounded official. 'I'm a policeman, Mr Anderson. It's my job to know these things.'

Inspector Mendez proudly puffed his chest up in agreement. David shook his head as if trying to clear his mind. 'But I still don't understand why you came all this way to see me if you don't have any news. Unless I'm being stupid, I can't see the point of it.'

'I'd like you to tell me why you decided to fly to Lisbon and join this particular ship? I take it that you had a good reason for not joining it at Southampton?'

David began showing his discomfort. 'All right. I'll tell you but you'll think I'm mad.'

'We'll see, shall we?' Bill Forward waited. 'Please go on.'

David tried to explain without sounding stupid. 'Well, as you know, I'm a freelance journalist. After I left you on the day I identified my brother's body, I went home. My girlfriend asked me all about it and I happened to tell her that you'd mentioned people that you wanted to interview. I'd written them down on a piece of paper and when she saw the name Verna Castle she told me that it was a ship that her cousin had been on.'

The inspector was annoyed. 'Then why didn't you call me and tell me that it was a ship and not a person? Have you any idea the time that's been wasted because of your withholding that information?'

David became nervous. 'I'm sorry. I know I should have told you.' He held his head in his hands. 'I really am sorry.'

Bill Forward relaxed. 'So tell me why you didn't, and why you came on this ship. Was it because of Susie Cunningham? Did you know that she was on this ship before you booked it up? And I want the truth, Mr Anderson.'

David sat up and tried to regain his composure. 'I intended telling you just as soon as I'd interviewed her. You see, I knew that an exclusive interview with a killer, especially a beautiful woman, would make me a lot of money. It was my one big chance. All I've done so far are local stories for local papers. This was an opportunity to get in with the nationals and open new doors.'

'And did you interview her?'

'When I spoke to her I realized that she didn't even know Paul was dead. So, I told her.'

'And?'

'She was stunned. Genuinely shattered by the news. She'd been to see him on Saturday evening and couldn't understand why she'd got no reply. When I told her why, she wasn't able to take it in. I may not be a policeman but I can tell you that Susie isn't a killer.'

Inspector Forward took his time. 'Then who do you think *did* kill your brother?'

'I don't know. I really don't. Unless it's that bloke you mentioned to me.'

'Julian Harper?'

'Yes. That's the one. Why don't you look for him?'

'Oh we did, Mr Anderson. Believe me, we did.' Bill Forward changed the subject. 'Are you and Miss Cunningham close, would you say?'

David gave a nervous laugh. 'I wish we were, inspector. How I wish we were. Susie is engaged to a passenger on board. They sit at the same table together in the dining room.'

Bill Forward became interested. 'Really? And what is this gentleman's name. Do you know?'

'Kerr. James Kerr.'

'Do you happen to know if they're on board at the moment?'

'I saw them walking round the shops in Malaga earlier. I don't know whether they're back yet or not.' David frowned. 'You don't think he's got something to do with Paul's death surely, inspector?'

'Just want a word with them both, that's all.' He became

businesslike. 'Thank you for your time, Mr Anderson. You won't be going ashore again today, will you?'

'Not today, no.'

Carlos Mendez got up and gave David an official nod.

David was relieved as the two policemen reached the door and he said jokingly, 'Not arresting me then, inspector?'

Bill Forward's mouth smiled but his eyes remained serious, 'Not at the moment, sir.'

As he and Carlos Mendez closed the door behind them, David began to wonder if he would be charged for withholding vital evidence and decided that he needed a stiff drink.

James and Susie arrived back on board mid-afternoon. She was still excited with her ring and wanted everyone to notice and admire it. As they made their way to the lift, Susie made a decision. 'You go on to your cabin, darling.' she told James. 'I can't wait till dinner to show Carol my ring.'

He enjoyed seeing her so happy. 'OK, but don't be long. I want to have you to myself for a while.'

She kissed his cheek. 'I won't be long. Promise.'

He watched her rush off thinking what a lucky man he was.

Susie arrived at Carol's door and paused for a moment to adjust her ring so that it would be seen to its best advantage. She was about to knock when she noticed the plastic key in the lock. She thought it unusual for Carol to leave it there and gave a gentle knock on the door. When she got no reply, a thought crossed her mind. Was Carol waiting for someone to call. A gentleman friend perhaps?

It was then she noticed that the plastic key was not like the one that she had. She removed it and when she looked more closely, she could see that it was like the keys used by the cabin stewards and chambermaids – the pass keys that allowed them access to any cabin. Replacing it, she remembered the feeling she'd had when someone had entered her own cabin, and was now wondering if that same person had got in to Carol's cabin. If anyone was inside going through personal things, she was determined to find out who they were.

Trying hard to keep her nerves under control, she knocked on the cabin door and after getting no response, opened it. There was no sign of Carol but she heard a noise from the bathroom and waited. When the bathroom door opened, Susie was shocked to see Carol, minus her hair. It was a grotesque sight and for a moment she was transfixed. Then she realized that what she was seeing wasn't Carol Mason. It was a man wearing women's clothing and make-up.

Surprised and puzzled by her presence, the man quickly rushed to the door and closed it. 'How did you get in?' he asked her.

Susie sat on the bed with her mouth open. It was Carol's voice but it was coming from a man. She was shaking as she asked, 'I don't understand. Who are you?'

He locked the door from the inside and tried to calm her, speaking in a quiet and friendly manner. 'Please don't worry. I have no intention of hurting you, Susie. You must believe that. How did you get in here?'

She was trying desperately to comprehend what was going on but was unable to hide her nervousness. 'The key was in the lock.'

'Careless me.' He unlocked the door and opened it enough to get his hand round and remove the key without being seen by any passer-by. Locking the door again he smiled. 'I think I'd better put my wig on, then you'll feel more comfortable and so will I. Promise you won't go? I want to explain all this to you.'

Susie was studying the face as she said, 'I won't leave.' Then suddenly it came to her. 'Good God! I've just realized where I saw your face before. The young man in one of the photographs in Paul's bedside cabinet.' Then as if trying to wake her senses she rubbed her forehead and asked, 'Are you a man dressed as a woman. Or a woman who dresses up as a man?' She sat there with a look of total confusion.

He stood in the bathroom putting on the beautiful dark wig that had framed Carol Mason's lovely face. Susie watched in total disbelief at what she was seeing. Within a few moments it was Carol Mason who returned and sat in a chair opposite her.

'Dear Susie, I really do want to explain everything to you and hope you will understand. Perhaps when you hear what I have to say, you will even forgive the wrong I have done. Maybe you will hate me. I don't know. But at least listen. Of all the people on this ship, I want you to understand what I have done and why.'

Susie began to feel comfortable again with the Carol she had known over these past few days. 'What do you mean, the wrong you've done?'

'Did you know that Paul is dead?'

'Yes. His brother told me.'

'Ah yes. My little lift boy.'

Susie showed surprise. 'How did you know that David was Paul's brother?'

Carol smiled. 'I had a phone call from England informing me of his identity. But more of that later. Let's go back a few months. You probably didn't know, but Paul was bisexual and changed from girls to men as the mood took him.'

Susie felt only revulsion, the way she had when she first suspected Paul's sexual practices. She shook her head and said quietly, 'Not at first, no.'

Carol continued. 'Paul and I met when he took on my friend Stephen as a client. There was something about Paul that had an effect on me. Call it chemistry. Anyway, I met him on the odd occasion and we became very close. So much so that when Stephen found out, it was impossible for me to live with him any longer. And so, I moved out and rented a house in Fulham. Then Stephen found another friend, Barry. They lived together and I was happy just seeing Paul now and then. I had no intention of moving in, even though he suggested it on more than one occasion. Then, out of the blue, Stephen telephoned me and said how he missed me and that he still wanted us to be friends. Anyway, the long and short of it is that we met from time to time just to chat and have a drink together. Then one day, he told me that Paul had got involved with a Dutchman who had lived in England for some time. Actually Susie, you met him.'

Susie said thoughtfully, 'De Jager?'

'That's him. Erik de Jager. A ruthless man who will use people to his own advantage and couldn't give a stuff about anyone but himself.' Carol licked her lips. 'I fancy a drink. How about you?'

Susie frowned as she nodded. 'I think I *need* one.'

'I've only got gin and tonic, I'm afraid. That OK?'

'Fine.'

Susie sat there trying to take in what she was being told, while Carol took the glasses and opened the refrigerator. She took out some ice and put it into the glasses, then half-filled them from a bottle of gin on the dressing table and topped them up with tonic water. Handing one to Susie, she apologized, 'No lemon, I'm afraid. Now, where was I?'

'You were talking about the Dutchman.'

'Oh yes. Well, I happened to be at Paul's one evening when he got rather drunk and begged me to stay the night. After a few more drinks he began telling me about you and how you had told him that you were going on a cruise. Then he told me that he and de Jager had arranged for you to unwittingly carry some of his ill-gotten gains on to the ship.'

'The bag!' Susie suddenly worked it out. 'There *was* something in it. I didn't imagine it. Somebody opened it and tore the lining, just as I thought they had.'

Carol was apologetic. 'That was me I'm afraid.'

'You?'

'I'll explain everything if you'll just let me tell you in my own way.' Looking at her watch she added, 'But I may have to leave in a few minutes. So I'll be as quick as I can.'

For the first time, Susie noticed two suitcases standing outside the wardrobe and put two and two together. 'You're leaving, aren't you? You're getting off the ship!'

Carol was becoming impatient. 'Please. Just listen and then perhaps you will understand. When I met de Jager it was as Julian Harper. He knew I was gay and made it clear that he also enjoyed male company from time to time, as did Paul. To be perfectly honest I disliked the man intensely, but he sounded me out regarding a scheme he was considering. It was for someone to travel on the ship as his representative and remove a package from your borrowed suitcase. Then meet his contact in Greece where packages would be exchanged and a bank account opened in the name of a phoney company.'

Engrossed by what she was hearing, Susie sat listening to every word her companion uttered.

'I told him I thought it was a wonderful idea and made it known that I would be interested in taking on the role of representative. He said he would discuss it with Paul and let me know. I saw this as the one chance I might have to fulfil my dream of becoming a woman. A *real* woman. Not just a bloody freak. You see, I have known that I was really female ever since I was five years old. But there is a law that says if you've got a dick then you're a man. Well, with the money, I can get rid of that piece of male appendage and become what nature meant me to be. You can't imagine what it has been like, Susie, always referred to as "that pretty boy". I hated being called that. Especially growing up in that bloody awful orphanage. Children can be such cruel little bastards.'

Susie was confused. 'But you told me that your parents were living in Albury and that they were wonderful.'

'Like me, I'm afraid that was a little deception. Oh, I had foster parents in Albury but they were worse than the orphanage, so I didn't stay there long. No, I never knew who my parents were, and now I couldn't give a monkey's who or what they were.'

'And when you told me that you had no money worries, that was another little deception?'

'I'm afraid so. If I'd had money I would have seen about having my operation long before now, I can assure you.'

'And you really want to go through with a complete sex change?'

'Since we first met have I been anything other than female as far as you were concerned?'

There was a slight laugh in Susie's voice. 'No. You've been very much a female, to be honest. Few women could turn heads the way you have.'

'Well, there's your answer.'

Susie became thoughtful and there was suspicion in her voice as she asked, 'Were you at Paul's when I called there to see him last Saturday?'

There was an uncomfortable moment before the answer came. 'Yes. I saw you ringing the outer bell as I waited for my bus. I wasn't sure if you'd seen me or not.'

'Oh yes, I saw you. But according to his brother, Paul was already dead when I arrived.' Susie plucked up her courage and said, 'You know who killed him, don't you?'

'Yes. I was there when it happened.'

Susie swallowed hard before asking, 'So, what *did* happen?'

'In sorting out some things for this trip, I found the keys that Paul had given me some time ago, which I had forgotten to give back to him. I telephoned and asked whether he wanted me to post them or not. He suggested that I took them over myself as he would like to see me before I sailed. I had already made plans to disappear for ever once I got to Piraeus, and decided that it would probably be the very last time I would ever see him anyway, so I went. I opened the door and let myself in and that's when I found Paul in his dressing gown having a terrible row with Barry Summers.'

Susie was confused. 'Who is Barry Summers?'

'Stephen's new boyfriend.'

Trying to make sense of it all, Susie said, 'And Stephen used to be your boyfriend, right?'

'Yes. Well the two of them had obviously been together in bed because Barry was still wearing only his underpants. The row was caused because, after making love together, Barry told Paul that he was probably HIV positive. Paul threw a punch at Barry and hit him hard in the face. Then Barry lost his temper and screamed abuse at Paul. Paul called him a filthy little bastard and suddenly, before I knew what was going on, Barry picked up a brass ornament and hit Paul at least twice across the back of his head. I grabbed the ornament from him and Paul fell to the floor. There was blood coming from his head and it was all like a horrible nightmare, with Barry sobbing and me in the middle of it all.'

'Didn't you call the police?'

'I was scared, Susie. Bloody scared. Then Barry pleaded for me not to call the police and it was while I was wiping the ornament clean that Barry said, if I called the police he'd tell them how I'd found him with Paul and killed him because I was jealous.'

Still trying to find some logic in the story, Susie asked, 'Why did you wipe the murder weapon?'

'I don't know why. I just did. Christ, Susie, I was nervous and scared. It was almost instinctive I guess. I like things to be tidy.' Carol smiled. 'That was a stupid thing to say. Sorry.'

Susie was becoming intrigued. 'So, go on. What happened?'

'While Barry was getting dressed I thought of a way to get rid of Julian Harper for good. Barry looked quite a bit like me. Same size. Same colouring. Anyway, he was still in a bad way, suffering from shock, so I told him to drive to Fulham and wait at the side of my house for me. No one would see him there. He said that he was on his way to see his mother but I convinced him that he could never go in the state he was in. When he was dressed I told him to leave by the back entrance of the building, which he did. I left by the front and didn't care who saw me because Julian Harper would soon vanish for good. That's why I didn't worry about you seeing me while I waited for my bus.'

Susie could see that Carol was beginning to enjoy reliving the experience and despite being aware of possible danger to herself, she wanted to know exactly what had happened. 'When you said that you had thought of a way of getting rid of Julian for good, what did you mean?'

Carol's eyes sparkled as she continued. 'When I got home, he was waiting in his car, looking like a zombie. I got him indoors and convinced him that the police could easily trace him by modern electronics and DNA tests, etc. He was terrified, and I told him that he should get out of his clothes because the police would be able to prove by testing them that he'd been at Paul's at the time of the killing. I took him into my bedroom and made him open the drawers to look for socks and underwear. Then he opened the wardrobe to see if there was anything that he fancied. His fingerprints were all over the place. I got him to do the same in the bathroom and kitchen. He was so nervous he did exactly what I wanted. He took a shower, then dressed. I got hold of all his clothes and told him that I would get rid of them for him. It was strange seeing him in my outfit. It was uncanny how alike we looked. I put his clothes in a wardrobe with some of my own and gave him a drink of water with some sleeping capsules. I told him they were pep pills and he believed me.

'We left the way we had come in, through the back door. My neighbours would be too busy watching some crap television programme to notice us. We got into the car but I drove. Although I hadn't driven for years, it was safer than having him fall asleep on me at the wheel. I parked just off Wimbledon common, knowing that it would be quite a while before it was treated as an old abandoned banger, which is what it was. I wiped the steering wheel clean and saw that Barry was fumbling in his pocket for something. When I got him out of the car he put a pill into his mouth and before I could stop him, a second one. I asked what they were and he told me they were ecstasy tablets. By that time we were near a large pond that I knew was quiet when it got dark. Barry was hardly able to stand. It was just as we got to the water's edge that he fell, face down into it. He gurgled for a moment then he went limp and still. I managed to put my wallet into the jacket pocket. It was empty apart from a medical card and odd papers. I knew that it would appear he had been robbed because no money was left in it. Then I took off my ring and put it on his finger and that was that. I didn't want him found too quickly, so I eased him into the roots of a bush.'

The calm way in which she had been told these facts made Susie shake her head in disbelief. 'You just let him die? Having planned the whole thing in cold blood?'

'Barry Summers was going to spread Aids to anyone he could before he died from it himself. His sort are evil and have no right to live. You may not like it, darling, but I've done society a favour.'

Susie almost laughed at the cool way she was being told all this. 'I cannot believe this is happening. And I suppose the man in Lisbon whose wife didn't understand him and the accident to your leg, all that was just lies too?'

'My Lisbon lover was a total lie, darling.'

'And the leg you injured as a child?'

Carol became less flamboyant. 'All true, I'm afraid. But I shall get the finest plastic surgeon there is to sort that out. I shall be able to afford it now.'

The telephone rang. Susie hoped it was for her. She needed time to recover from the shock of learning Carol's secret. 'That might be James. He'll be wondering what's keeping me.'

Carol picked up the receiver. 'Hello … Yes it is … Thank you. If you could get someone to collect my bags … He's on his way? … Oh lovely.' She hung up. 'By the way. Why did you come to see me?'

Holding out her hand, Susie indicated the ring. 'I came to show you this, but suddenly all my enthusiasm to show it off has gone.'

Admiring the ring Carol had a warm smile. 'You must never lose your enthusiasm, darling. You're a lovely girl, Susie. I hope you will be very happy. I envy you terribly. You cannot imagine what it's like to want a man but not be able to let him see you undressed, let alone get into bed with you. But once I have my operation I shall make up for lost time.' A broad grin appeared. 'Just think, I shall be able to enjoy sex without having to worry about periods or producing children.' She took a large envelope from her bag and placed it on the dressing table. 'I shall be leaving in a moment and would be grateful if you kept our conversation between ourselves for a while. Even five minutes would be a help.'

'But you killed a man. Don't you feel anything?'

'He killed himself, darling. Those ecstasy tablets were his idea.'

'How can you be so uncaring about it all? You admitted to me that you set out to kill him. You gave him some sleeping capsules and changed his clothes. Everything that you have done relied on this Barry being dead.'

'True. But would I have actually seen it through had he not taken those tablets? We'll never know will we? Oh, by the way, there's a police inspector on board and he will no doubt be speaking to you. Please see that he gets that envelope. I've explained everything in the letter.'

Susie was confused. 'Why would he want to speak to me?'

'Just routine, darling. Worry not. It's all in the letter. Trust me. Oh, one other thing. There's a young officer named Peter. Fancies me like mad. Even came to my cabin when he was off duty. If he should enquire about me, tell him I had to visit a sick aunt or something. He's a sweet boy.' She took the two passports from her bag and checked them.

Susie watched with great fascination. 'Why have you got two passports?'

'One for me, Carol Mason. The other one is for future use darling.' She returned them to her bag. 'There. Now I shall leave the ship as Carol. And once ashore, who knows?'

There was a knock at the door. Susie wasn't sure what she should do and decided to stay where she was. Carol went to the door. 'That will be the boy for the bags.'

As Carol opened the door she saw James standing there with Inspector Forward. Carol smiled and appeared quite calm.

'James darling. Susie hoped it would be you. Who's your handsome friend?'

'This is Detective Inspector Forward. This is Carol Mason, inspector.'

James was amused at the way Carol gave a sexy look at the policeman. 'Watch her, inspector. She's a man eater.'

'Only when I'm hungry, darling.'

At that moment the steward arrived. 'Are these the bags to go, miss?'

'Just those two. I'll bring this one.' She picked up the holdall.

Bill Forward was taken aback by the dark-haired beauty and showed it. 'Leaving already, Miss Mason?'

'Afraid so, inspector. A sick relative I'm very fond of.'

'I'm sorry.' Bill Forward stood back from the door. 'I hope you find them better when you get back.'

'Thank you. Goodbye, James. Take care of your lovely girl. And you take care of him, Susie. In this nasty world we all need someone to love.' The look that she gave Susie was almost a plea for her silence. 'Ciao everyone.'

Susie knew that she had just seen a great performance but would never be able to live with herself if she didn't speak to the inspector. She was just about to say something when there was a message over the public address system: 'Would Mr Forward, recently arrived from London, please contact the radio room for an incoming call?'

Bill Forward turned to go. 'That's for me. We never like to use our official title in situations like this. Don't want people worried about a policeman being on board. If you will excuse me I'll see you in your cabin in a few minutes, Miss Cunningham. Inspector Mendez will keep you company while I'm gone.'

It wasn't until he left that Susie was aware of another policeman out in the corridor. Now, she didn't know what to do about Carol or the letter and James could see that she was perturbed. 'What is it, darling? Something the matter?'

'Yes. I have to talk to you. Can we close the door?'

James began to close it and smiled at Carlos Mendez. 'Can my fiancée and I be alone for a moment, please?'

Mendez nodded. 'Of course. I shall be here.'

As soon as James had closed the door, Susie began trying to explain to him what had just taken place between Carol and herself. She hadn't got far with her story before James interrupted her. 'Are you telling me that Carol is a *man*!'

'I know it sounds ridiculous but if you had seen her, him, without that wig you'd know it was true. James darling, I think I know why the inspector wants to see me.' She explained about her visit to see Paul in order to end what had been a brief romantic interlude. And while she was explaining how her involvement with Paul had come about, she knew that despite feeling terrible, the truth was now her only way out of the mess she was in.

James listened to her and when she had finished, looked at her face and kissed the tears that had appeared. 'I love you, Susie. The past is past. It's now and the rest of our lives that are important. But I think we must tell the inspector and give him the letter. Come on, darling. We'd better get back to your cabin before he sends out a search party.'

Returning his smile, Susie realized how lucky she was that James hadn't walked out on her. Opening the cabin door, they led the way back to B deck with Inspector Mendez following.

After a few minutes, Bill Forward arrived at cabin B70 and spoke to Mendez who was waiting outside. The inspector was not in the best of moods. 'That was my sergeant. He went to inform a Mr Stephen Conley that his live-in lover had been found dead in a lake, only to discover that he'd already been told. And now he's gone and topped himself.'

Mendez looked confused. 'Topped?'

'Oh, it's another name for committing suicide. I tell you, Carlos, this case is becoming a bloody nightmare. Let's see what Miss Cunningham has to say for herself.' He knocked, and James opened the door.

'Come in, inspector.'

As the two policemen entered the cabin, Bill Forward explained, 'Inspector Mendez has to be present during any interview. It's part of international law, so I hope you don't mind, Miss Cunningham?'

'No. Of course not. And I hope it's all right for James to be present?'

'As you wish. Now the purpose of this interview is to try and establish what you were doing at—'

'I know why you're here, inspector,' Susie interrupted. 'And I think I can save you a lot of time if I tell you that Carol Mason will have left the ship by now and is probably travelling as fast as she can from the Malaga area.'

Inspector Forward showed surprise. 'I know that Miss Mason has left the ship. I was there when her bags were taken. I don't quite see what her leaving the ship has got to do with my reason for speaking to you, Miss Cunningham.'

Susie became nervous and swallowed hard before answering. 'Inspector, I know it will be hard for you to accept, but Carol Mason is a man.'

Bill Forward screwed up his face in disbelief. 'You're telling me that the beautiful woman I saw was a man! Are you serious?'

James came to Susie's defence. 'It's the truth, inspector. I was fooled too, just as everyone else was.'

The inspectors looked at each other with scepticism and it was Mendez who asked, 'The lady whose cabin we found you in was not a lady? Is that what you are asking us to believe, señor?'

James realized it sounded ridiculous but tried convincing the two policeman. 'Susie actually saw her without the wig. I mean him without the wig. Tell them, Susie.'

'It's true. One minute I was looking at a man in woman's make-up and clothes. The next moment it was Carol again. But the name isn't Carol. It's Julian Harper. At least, that's what he said.'

Inspector Forward was momentarily shocked. Then turning to Mendez he said, 'Quick! Get down to the gangway and see if anyone noticed Carol Mason leave and whether she took a taxi or had a car waiting. That woman has to be stopped. Give out her description to your people. Whatever happens we've got to find her!'

Mendez hurried from the cabin without saying a word.

Inspector Forward spoke in an official tone. 'I want you two to remain here. Is that understood?'

Susie picked up the envelope from the dressing table

and gave it to him. 'Carol asked me to give you this. She said that it would explain everything.'

He took the envelope and hurried after Inspector Mendez.

Susie sat down on the edge of the bed and James sat next to her. He put his arm around her. 'Don't worry, darling. They'll soon find her. I mean him. I cannot get used to Carol being a him. But now that we know the truth, it explains why she behaved the way she did. Why there were always those sexually suggestive remarks and the apparent interest in young men. Looking at it from a medical point of view, Carol Mason's sex life must have been terribly frustrating. Quite awful in fact.'

Susie was staring thoughtfully. 'It's funny, but in a way I hope they never find her. I'm actually beginning to feel sorry for her. Does that sound dreadful?'

James shook his head. 'Not really. I know what you mean. It's certainly going to seem very strange without seeing that face across the table.'

'Life was certainly never dull with Carol around. In a funny way, I'm really going to miss her,' said Susie.

'Don't you mean him?' James corrected her. 'It's a man that we're talking about.'

'Is it?' she said doubtfully. 'I think you'll find that she is much more female than you think.'

'What do you mean?'

She kissed him tenderly on his cheek. 'I'll tell you all about it later.' Susie smiled and added, 'I think we should keep the truth from Lionel and Sybil. I have a feeling they wouldn't understand. Let's just say that she had a gentleman from England who flew all the way here, just to take her back with him.'

James gave a quizzical look. Then he jokingly said, 'Well, at least it's the truth. And it would never do to lie to the Westons. With Lionel being a man of the Church it would be very wrong to do that.'

Susie nodded in agreement. 'Of course it would. Sybil is sure to be delighted that Carol is off the ship. But I don't think Lionel will be. In fact, he will probably be upset at her leaving. I think the reverend secretly fancied her.'

James gave her a reprimanding look, and then both he and Susie began laughing at the thought.

After reading Julian Harper's letter, which proved to be a statement of confession, Inspector Forward was satisfied with Susie's account of her visit to Paul Anderson's flat. When he left the *Verna Castle*, he wished James and Susie good luck for the future.

He returned to England, leaving Inspector Mendez with the task of trying to find Julian Harper, alias Carol Mason, and hopefully arranging extradition in order to get his man back on British soil.

The conversation at dinner was all about the enigmatic Ms Mason, and Sybil made it clear that she was convinced the man who had flown out to take her back with him was in reality her husband. She was sure Carol Mason was a loose woman who didn't know the meaning of the word faithful, and had always been of the opinion that there was something unsavoury about her. The Reverend Lionel would have disagreed with his wife but preferred the quiet life and said nothing, while James and Susie agreed with Sybil that she was probably right.

David Anderson made friends with one of the dancers

in the show on board, and spent every night either watching her on stage or entertaining her in his cabin on her nights off. He would remain unaware that he was a beneficiary of his brother Paul's will, until he returned home.

Mark Sutherland made a phone call to his Greek agent in Athens, for whom he was to begin work immediately he had finished his contract with a Greek fashion house. He was now confirming the deal with the agent and everything was satisfactory. Mark would stay at a large house a few miles outside Athens. He was told that the house would also be the location for the videos he would make. His agent then told him, in some detail, about the beautiful girls he had contracted for Mark to work with. As he listened to the description of each girl, he became excited at the thought of having sex with them. Even though most people condemned any sort of pornography, Mark convinced himself that what he did would enhance other people's sex lives while they watched him. Besides which, there was big money to be made and Mark wanted to make it before he became too old for the work.

Just before lunch the following day, James received the call from his partner, Doctor Philip Dayton. Susie waited anxiously while he went to the radio room to take it. When he returned to her he was all smiles. 'Good news, darling. Mr Walter Mathews has examined your mother and taken her off all the drugs prescribed by Leddington-White.'

Her face lit up. 'And?'

'He doesn't think your mother ever had Alzheimer's. He is of the opinion that she was originally suffering from a form of mental blackouts which caused temporary memory loss. This is common in people of middle age and upwards where any kind of stress or anxiety is allowed to exist over a long period. Can you think of anything that might have given rise to such symptoms?'

'Only the way my stepfather treated her. He's enough to make anyone ill.'

'Anyway, she's on the mend. They think that with a bit of luck, she will be more like her normal self in two or three weeks. Walter Mathews is giving her all the attention that she needs to get well.'

Susie closed her eyes as if saying a private prayer. When she opened them again they were moist from tears of joy. She threw her arms around her fiancé and whispered several times, 'Thank you. Thank you.'

James was happy for her and cuddled her close to him. 'Why don't we send her a postcard and tell her that we are having a wonderful time and that I can't wait to meet her. Then we can enjoy the rest of our cruise, knowing that by the time we get home, she should be well on the mend.'

Susie nodded in agreement and said, 'Stay with me tonight.'

He held her extra close and whispered, 'And every night from now on.'

EPILOGUE

It was almost six months later that Susie and her mother were busy putting the final touches to the house that James had purchased on the edge of Wimbledon common.

Susie was now Mrs Kerr and her mother had moved into what had once been the servants' quarters. She and her daughter were happy being together again, just like the days before her mother's illness. And while James was attending surgery, he was happy in the knowledge that his wife wasn't alone.

Susie's stepfather remained at his own house and was not seen or heard of again.

Among the many cards, welcoming them to their new home, was a letter that had been forwarded on from Susie's flat. It had been readdressed, having been sent care of: Lion Castle Shipping Line, Dover. The postmark was from Venice and had been franked ten days earlier. Susie opened the envelope and read the contents with great interest. It read:

My dear lovers,
I do hope this reaches you and that you are still happy
together. I think of you often and while I was having

my operation, I kept wondering whether you had married and if you thought of me now and then. Well, the op was a great success and so now we are all girls together, Susie. The hormones are working a treat and I hardly ever need a razor these days, thank God.... That bloody barber's rash needed so much make-up.

Ever hear anything of the reverend and his keeper? Silly to ask because you can't possibly answer. Shame that. I'd really like to know all your news, but things being as they are, I have to keep my whereabouts hush hush. I have had a lovely few days here in Venice with a wonderful man. Not only is he handsome but rich with it. (Can this be true love I ask myself?) You may be interested to know that the Dutchman dropped dead a few weeks ago. Poor thing couldn't adjust to the fact that someone had run off with all his contraband. Well, at least there won't be any more drugs getting into England via him! I did so enjoy your company, Susie. Talking to you made me feel like a new woman. (And so I thought I'd become one!)

Love to you both.
Be Happy. Always.
Ciao.
A friend
x x x